UNJUSTIFIED 🔗 DEMANDS

BAYLEE ROSE

UNJUSTIFIED
⛓
DEMANDS

© 2016 Baylee Rose

Cover Design:

Yoly Cortez with Cormar Covers

Cover Photography:

Eric David Battershell

Cover Models:

Ani Saliasi & Anna Medvedeva

Formatting and Editing:

Daryl Banner

DEDICATION

To everyone who had a dream and never gave up.

Always believe.

Baylee

CONTENTS

"Boss, we got a problem."

I'm looking out over the one-way window of my upstairs office that shows the bar and dance floor below. Here I was, thinking it was going to be a slow night. I own one of the premiere night spots in Miami, and for the most part, things run smoothly. I have my fingers in a lot of pots though, so I can't help but worry about what Joe deems as a *problem*.

"What's up, Joe?" Big Joe is my right hand and my number one bouncer. He can usually handle anything, so for him to come to me is enough to set off warning bells. I swivel my chair back around to look at him.

"That kid you caught trying to sell his shit in the club last week?"

"Yeah?"

"He's got family."

"I fail to see why this concerns me, Joe."

It sounds cold. Then again, I am fucking cold. Still, I gave the kid two chances to stop pushing his crap in my club. He didn't listen. The way I see it, three strikes and you're out. I'd already been more lenient with him than I would be others. He was so fucking young. Twenty-one. *Young, dumb, and full of cum.* Hell, at forty-two, I'm starting to think I'm too damned old to be doing this job anymore. I have money—more than enough money. Maybe I should just seek out some sandy beach out of the country and call it a day. Greece, my mother's family was from there. Even if my mother was a fucking bitch, maybe I'll find some affinity for the country.

"His sister's been making waves," he tells me.

"Again, why do I care?" I ask, taking a drink of my Scotch. It's aged perfectly and the burn soothes me going down.

"She's been talking to the cops."

"Fucking hell. What does she know?"

"Not a lot. But you know the badges. They hear your name and they're going to come running."

I sigh. He's not wrong. They just hear the name Roman Anthes and they come poking around, descending on my club, my company, and any holdings I have. Since I'm trying to broker a deal to get into bed with the Russians, that could be disastrous right now.

"Where is this sister?"

"That's just it, boss. You just hired her."

"I haven't hired anyone here at the club in months," I argue. I'm very careful about the workers I hire here. I make sure I have them all vetted carefully and meticulously.

"Not here. She started work at the Dive."

"Waitress?" The Dive is a strip joint on the edge of a low rent side of town. I won the fucking thing in a card game. Had plans for selling it off, just haven't got around to it yet.

"Dancer. You gave Yoly the okay to hire her a couple of weeks ago. She's starting to get pretty popular. Yo says business has tripled since she started."

"Does she have any idea who she works for?"

"Don't see how she could, boss. No one knows you own the Dive, and those papers are buried and tangled so deep, even the feds couldn't find them."

"Do you have her file?"

"Sure thing." He hands a plain manila folder to me and I let it stay on my desk, thinking.

"What do we have on her?" I ask, opening the folder and

moving my fingers over the glossy 5 by 7 picture stapled to the application. It's a blonde with medium-length hair which is cut to curl toward her face and accent her strong cheekbones. Her eyes are violet. I never knew they made eyes that color. I have all my dancers photographed in nothing but their underwear, and she's definitely got the body to make men beg. I thumb through the rest of it quickly.

"Just what's in the file, boss. Well, that and obviously her affection for her brother."

"What did we do with the little fucker?" I ask him. My eyes keep going back to the photo of the blonde.

"He's at the warehouse. You have him in one of the containers."

"So, not yet dead?"

"No, but only because Bruno has been out for his kid's surgery."

"How is Thomas?"

"It was a success, thanks to your generosity. Bruno says they even said Thomas would be able to walk after some therapy."

"Good, good. Tell Bruno to hold off. The kid might prove to be useful."

"What are you thinking?"

"I'm thinking the asshole might yet prove of use to me," I tell him without expanding. He knows me well enough that he just closes the door, leaving me to my thoughts.

Ana Stevens. The pretty blonde dancer has no idea what trouble she just landed into. I reach down and adjust my cock because the son of a bitch has been rock hard since I laid eyes on Ana's picture. Why does it suddenly feel like, despite everything, my day is looking up?

Ana

I hate everything about this club. Walking through the front doors makes me feel like I'm being locked in a prison. The staring begins immediately. Men following me with their eyes, watching every move I make. I'm not a person; I'm a piece of meat, an image they want to jerk off to, a notch on their bedpost they can brag about.

Does that sound conceited? Maybe. There's a difference between knowing you appeal to men and feeling beautiful. I feel *tired*. At twenty-six, I'm so damned exhausted of living, but I ignore it. I don't have a choice.

"Hey, Ana! Looking good tonight," Joe, the sometimes-bouncer at The Dive, hollers out. I smile at him, my hand squeezing his big, scarred, beefy shoulder before walking on back to the private area.

I know the way by heart, which is good, because my vision is limited. My eyes are hidden behind my dark sunglasses. It doesn't matter that I'm inside. I play a role, wrapping myself in a package that makes me a mystery, all designed to make men interested. They see something unobtainable.

In truth, the sunglasses hide the bags under my eyes until I get in the dressing room so Joyce can cover them in makeup. Not being able to sleep is a bitch.

I sit down at the makeup table with a heavy sigh, letting my overnight bag I keep my shit in fall to the floor. Joyce immediately comes over and starts the major tease job she always does on my hair. I hate it. I usually wear my hair simple and straight. Hell, most of the time I tie it in a messy knot and go on. But I make money off of being the Ice Queen who every man wants to melt, so I let Joyce have her way.

"You're late," she chastises.

"Been out looking for Allen."

"Still no luck?"

"None. I'm starting to lose hope, J."

I hate having this conversation. I like Joyce. She's been good to me, and talking about this stuff with her seems wrong. When she squeezes my shoulder tight in response, our eyes meet in the makeup mirror. We're so different, but she's like the mom I've never had. She's fifty-two but looks to be in her early forties. She has this brown curly hair that she always has styled and teased yet clipped up out of her way. Joyce has these pretty green eyes with flecks of gold in them and they see far more than people give her credit for.

"If you don't start sleeping, it's going to affect your show, Ana."

"I know. I tried."

"Might have worked if you'd quit crying over that damn brother of yours."

She's not wrong. Still, I can't seem to stop the tears. I lost Allen a year ago in every way that mattered. That doesn't mean that having him missing is any easier. He's been gone for over a month now. He's disappeared before, but never this long.

"He's my responsibility," I tell her, the truth of that lodging in my stomach.

"Yeah, but he's killing you."

"I can't help it."

"I know, doll. I know. Let's see what magic ol' Joyce can work to hide those bags," she says with a sigh, going to work on my face.

Twenty minutes later, Joyce manages to pull off a minor

miracle and make me look good. I go to the wings of the stage and wait for my cue. Once I'm out there, I do my best to let everything go. I let the music take over and go through my routine like a well-seasoned veteran. I should be; I've been dancing for nine years now. I started before I was legal. It's amazing what fake IDs and bosses who don't give a fuck will get you. I can work the pole and I can shake the ass. I can do everything needed to make men horny and women beg for more. I can even look like I'm enjoying it when inside I'm slowly withering away. My set ends with yelling for more. I never give them that. Isn't that an age old adage? Always leave them wanting more? I blow them a kiss and walk off, appearing unconcerned that my breasts are completely bare as my ass, except for a small string of material. Big Joe puts the white silk robe around me and I lean up to kiss his cheek.

"Thanks, big guy," I tell him. He knows I hate being nude. In fact, I hate everything about dancing. I did it for a few months when I hit sixteen. I needed the money to keep a roof over our heads because our strung-out mother was spending every dime she could on her next hit. *You have to do what you have to do.* When mom almost overdosed and did permanent damage to herself, I got free of her, in a way, and found new paths. Allen never bothered, instead following in mom's footsteps. So here I am, dancing and trying to save my brother who is already too far gone.

"Another great show as always, Ana."

I squeeze his arm like I always do and disappear to my dressing room. I have one more set to do tonight, and then I can leave. I need to try and search for Allen some more, or try old contacts I haven't used in years. I can't remember the last time I've slept. My mind churns through all the chaos that is my life and just won't shut down long enough to allow sleep.

I sit down at the chair in front of my dressing table. Joyce hands me a cigarette and a light, which I gratefully take. It's a routine of mine. I always have a smoke after I dance. The nicotine helps me to calm. It's the only crutch I allow myself. I take a drag and my head goes back, eyes closing, and I try my best to squash down the panic over Allen. I've tuned out the room, so when a large hand wearing one lone insignia ring on his finger reaches over and takes away the cigarette, I'm unprepared.

"Sorry, you're not supposed to be back here," I say, annoyed, and look around for Joyce to signal for Joe. "And can I please have my cigarette back?"

"No."

"No?" I ask the big tall mountain of a man. He's easily six foot five, but he's broad as a house. He's got dark hair that's cut close to his head in the back and a little longer on top, dark eyes, and he wears a suit that probably cost more than my entire budget for food did the last two months combined. He screams money. Worse, he screams danger.

"My woman doesn't smoke. That was your last one."

"Your woman?" I ask. Something about the way he says that seems like it's a done deal in his mind and my heart speeds up against my chest. Fuck. *Where is Joe?* "Listen, I don't know who you think you are, but—"

"That's easy, Ana. I own you," he answers, and his words strike fear deep inside of me.

So much for keeping my head down and not drawing any attention.

3

I watch her eyes dilate with my announcement. Her breathing hitches in her chest. *Fear.* It can be the biggest aphrodisiac there is. At least for me. Ana's picture didn't do her justice. She's fucking delicious. A tad too skinny, but she has a plump round ass that I plan to leave pink with my handprints, and tits that beg a man to fill his mouth with them and bite, marking them. Strangely enough, the part of her body that draws most of my attention is her neck. It's long and slender, the delicate bones and corded muscle calling to the animal inside of me, and I want to clamp my teeth there every fucking day, leaving a bruise to broadcast to any fucking person around, man or woman, that she's taken. My dick, the stupid fuck, jerks again. He's been standing at attention ever since I saw Ana's picture, and being this close to her is just making it worse.

"Ready to go?" I ask, my voice brusque. I'm so fucking hard it's painful. I plan on pounding into that body and leaving her so sore, she won't walk right for a week. It will serve her right for tying my dick up in knots.

"Go?"

"Yeah, pet, we have somewhere we need to go."

"I'm not going anywhere with you. I don't know you. If you don't leave right now, I'll call Big Joe in here to deal with you," she huffs, and those eyes grab my attention. Her file said violet, and maybe they are, but right now I'd swear I could see sparks of silver. I've never seen anything like them before, and I've always been the kind of man who likes to collect rare finds.

"Go ahead, call Joe," I dare her.

That seems to take her back for a moment. "Joe!" she calls, her voice thick with panic.

"Yeah, Ana?" Joe says, coming back through the small area that leads to the dressing room. "Oh! Hey, Mr. Anthes. I didn't know you'd be here tonight," he adds.

My eyes never leave Ana's. I see the moment that recognition flares in Ana's eyes.

"You're Mr. Anthes?" she asks in a whisper.

The words reach me, but barely. I'm enjoying the way her throat muscles move as she swallows. I feel my cock stretch against my slacks, demanding release. In my head, I'm picturing holding onto Ana's blonde mane and force-feeding her my cock, making her take me all the way back, stretching that pretty little throat just before she swallows down my cum.

"I am," I confirm, knowing that even if she doesn't know me personally, she will recognize the name that signs her paychecks. I grab the coat folded over her small dressing table when she stands. "Put this on. We have business to discuss."

"Business?" Her hand goes up to her throat. I don't bother answering her; instead, I hold the coat for her to slide into. "What kind of business, Mr. Anthes?" she asks.

She looks like a small, frightened doe who's just been discovered by the hunter, who has her in his sights and his gun loaded. My mouth twists in a wry smile. It's an accurate analogy because she is my prey and I'm definitely loaded and ready to fire into her—or maybe on her.

"Now, Ana," I order, and it could be my imagination, but I see a shiver of awareness run through her body.

"I can't leave," she protests, standing. "I have another set."

"No, I don't believe you do. Joe? Get one of the other girls to fill in for Ana."

"Sure thing, boss. Libby can do it."

"I can't afford to take off." I ignore her answer. "I need to put my clothes on," she says, holding on tightly to the belt of her robe.

"I'd prefer you didn't," I tell her because I just plan on ripping them off of her soon. "Now put on your coat and let's go. You've kept me waiting long enough."

"Listen, Mr. Anthes, boss or not, I'm not leaving until I get dressed. Further, I don't think I'm stepping foot outside of this club until you tell me where we're going."

I look at her then. She's completely serious. It's a glitch in my plan that I didn't foresee. Usually, women know who I am and are only too thrilled to do what I order. The fact that Ana doesn't, irritates and intrigues me all at once. It is... *unexpected*.

"Everyone out." I order, and the room goes still. Within just a matter of moments, everyone that had been viewing my conversation with Ana is gone. The last to leave is Joe, and as the door shuts behind him, I can see reality sink in on Ana.

"What are you doing?"

"Waiting for you to get dressed so we can leave. You have two minutes."

"I can't get dressed with you in here!" I ignore her and lean against the closed door with my arms folded and wait. "You need to leave," she insists again, the nerves coming through her voice loud and clear. It's clear she's not going to fall into my hands easily. I could use her brother as leverage, but I find myself reluctant to do that, even now. *Interesting.*

I don't know what it is about Ana. Normally I wouldn't touch one of the dancers, or hell, any of the women that work for me. I'm careful about the women I choose. I have no explanation other than I want her and I always get what I want. Time to make that clear.

"Take off the robe, Ana."

She looks around the room helplessly.

"I—"

"Take. It. Off."

"I will not. Why on earth would I?"

"Because I ordered you to," I tell her, taking a step closer. This might be more fun than I anticipated.

4
Ana

"Then I quit. I'll get my things and leave," I tell him, completely bluffing. I hear something in my voice. *Something I don't want to put a name to.* He walks towards me ... slowly, stealthily. He reminds me of a mountain lion on the prowl for its prey. The problem is, I'm the prey in the scenario and my legs seem to have become deadweights refusing to move. He stops when he gets right in front of me. He towers over me and I'm having trouble catching my breath.

"Take it off, Ana," he orders again, but this order isn't like the other. This order is soft and seductive. His voice is hoarse and needy like a lover's, and when he says my name, small shivers of awareness run through my body.

"Why?"

"I want to see," he says, which seems absurd because I was just naked onstage.

"What's going on?" I ask, confused about why my body feels... *excited.* There are so many undercurrents between us, it seems surreal. Attracting Roman Anthes's attention should be the last thing in the world I want, so why am I enjoying it?

"You caught my eye," he says, as if that explains everything. Maybe it does.

It doesn't explain my reaction to him, however.

He's standing right in front of me. His large body overshadows me, making my five-foot-five frame feel small. His shoulders are so broad that even under his expensive suit you can tell he's solid muscle. His dark hair is so black, the light in the room seems to absorb it so that it casts a glow around him. He's that commanding. I instantly know he could color everything around him, take any room or situation over. *Take me over.* I should fear that, and on some level I do. It also excites me. The blood runs through my body and my pulse thrums as if I just ran fifty miles nonstop. His eyes are deep pools of blue, but not just any color of blue; these shine like the sky on a hot cloudless summer day. They warm you, and I do mean that literally. I feel the heat from him. My body feels *hot* and he's most definitely the source. So hot that, without thinking, I come close to pulling the collar of my robe away from my body. At the last moment, I stop myself and lamely rub the side of my neck instead, unable to tear my eyes away from him.

"Mr. Anthes," I start, but my voice is quiet. I can barely hear it over the way my heart is pounding against my chest. Can he hear? I try to concentrate to make my words clearer, louder. "I don't know what that means," I tell him, not sure I'm succeeding with the whole "louder" thing. In fact, I'm almost positive I'm hyperventilating. Can you faint from too much ... *everything*? Roman is *too much*, period, dot, and end of sentence.

His fingers move to my hand and glide slowly up my neck, his thumb brushing the side of my face. The touch isn't gentle, but it has that quality. I get the feeling Roman doesn't *do* gentle. His fingers curve into my hair and, for a split second, I forget to breathe. He studies my face and I'm afraid I'm giving away more than I mean to. I feel his fingers at the pulse point on my neck and I know he can feel how it's beating out of control. His eyes move over my flushed face, then lower to my breasts. I want to bring my arms up to cover them because my robe is thin, but I can't because he's so close. I'm painfully aware of how my nipples are erect against the fabric. I'd like to say it's because of the coolness of the room, but I can't. I bite my lip to keep from begging him to do something. I hope it would be demanding he leaves, but in all honesty, that's doubtful. *What is going on with me?*

"Are you a virgin, Ana?" he asks, and the bluntness of the question jars me so much that my head jerks back in reaction.

"I can't believe..."

"Answer the question, Ana." Again, that commanding tone drips from his tongue and pours over me, and I react in a way that surprises me: I *obey* him. I'm submissive in the bedroom by nature, but Roman is the first man to ever have the power to make me follow his lead outside of the bedroom, and without effort. It's madness, and I do my best to pull myself away from the hypnotic effect he has on me.

"No." I tell him, and I see his eyes flash. It's like an emotion skitters through them and causes the color to deepen. What would they do when he's touching a woman? Or when he's making love to her? It might be best if I don't think of that. *Ever.*

"Then why are you so opposed to me seeing you when the entire room outside just saw the same thing?"

"They were strangers," I whisper inanely. It's hard to explain how I differentiate myself from the room when I dance and how I can zone everything out except the music and the steps.

"But then, so am I Ana."

"It's different," I defend.

"How?"

"They don't matter," I tell him, immediately wanting to kick myself. What happened to the woman who is self-controlled and can handle any situation? She's gone right now for sure, because that didn't come out how I meant it to. "I mean, it's not that you matter either. When I dance, there is distance. I don't focus on anyone. One-on-one is different. It's why I don't do private dances. Taking my clothes off for a man is reserved for someone I'm dating, someone I care about."

I'm blathering on and the embarrassment infuses deeper into my face, the heat from it coming off of me in waves so that I know it's there.

I try to pull away because I've made a big enough fool out of myself. He doesn't let me. Instead, his hold increases in strength and he pulls me into him. I fall awkwardly against him. His hand locks against my neck. I look into his eyes, which are just a breath away from mine. "Mr. Anth—"

That's all I get out before his lips crash against mine. His are firm, but soft at the same time. His tongue slips through my lips and instantly finds mine. For a moment I don't respond, too shocked to move, but then slowly it all hits me: the feel of his rough hand against my neck and face, the way he towers over me and makes me feel small, the sweet taste of his mouth, the way his tongue is searching mine out, and most importantly, the way his body crushes up against me—*solid, determined, warm.* I give in with a moan, pushing into him and wanting more. My tongue finds his and they dance, wrapping around each other in their fight for supremacy. I feel one of his hands move to my ass, pushing under the robe and cupping it as if we weren't in the middle of a club. I should stop him, but his fingers flex into my ass cheek and the feel of that is so good that combined with his kiss, I'm too lost in all that is him to even think of calling a halt.

"You're a hell of a kisser, Ana Stevens," he whispers once he pulls away. He moves away slightly and places a gentle peck against my forehead before retreating. My body leans towards his at first, not wanting him to go, but I manage to stop before I make too big of a fool of myself.

"That shouldn't have happened," I tell him.

He looks at me for a minute as if searching for something. I have no idea if he finds it. I figure he doesn't because he turns away from me. I just stand there stupidly as he walks away.

"I don't date," he mutters, his back still to me as he opens the door.

I'm sure he doesn't need to. Women probably throw themselves at his feet. He has that god-like persona. He's beautiful and commanding. He has more money than I will see in my lifetime. He's definitely dark and dangerous, and he has that forbidden vibe—especially to me. Women must flock to him. All of that, added into the way he kisses? I fight back the urge to tell him I'll go with him. For just one more taste of him, I think I'd agree to almost anything. *He's that addicting.* I shake my head out of the fog he's woven around it. This is stupid. I do not fit into Roman's world; even trying would destroy me. Of that, I'm sure.

"I'll be out in an hour, Mr. Anthes," I bluff. I can't leave because I have to find Allen. My voice is raw but solid, bringing the conversation back to the business at hand.

"There's no need, Ana. You may remain dancing, at least until I decide what I'm going to do with you."

What he's going to do with me? Now *that's* something to worry about. I can hear Paul bitch at me now for taking chances. "What do you—"

"I'll see you soon, pet," he says over his shoulder before he disappears.

Pet?

I'm left staring after him like a deer caught in the headlights of a fast-moving car. *I hope I survive the crash.*

5
Roman

Two Weeks Later

I sit in the back of the room watching the dance floor through the smoke. I shake the ice in my glass before downing the last of my scotch. I may own the Dive, but it's not my scene. I keep it to launder my money through. It serves a purpose, just like most things in my life.

That's not the reason I'm here tonight. I'm here for Ana. I should have just walked away. I spent a week convincing myself of that. I spent the following week trying to replace her. That was a colossal failure. I couldn't even get it up. I'd kiss a girl and instead of getting turned on, I kept remembering the feel of Ana's body, the taste of her mouth and wanting more of her, because apparently no one else will work. It's all I can seem to think about. Hell, I even jacked off to the memory of our kiss last night. A fucking kiss has me harder than I've been since I was a young kid wet behind the ears.

Now, the plan is to fuck her out of my system. Ana will be mine—*one way or another*. I still hesitate to use the brother, but I might if she forces my hand.

She is even more beautiful tonight. Her blonde hair is short, falling down in a straight, silky and sleek golden halo at her shoulders. It's beautiful, but too controlled. *In too much order.* It's not hard to imagine it rumbled and messed up in bed, though. Her whole body screams sex, with the way her hips move and the way her legs tighten against the pole as she gyrates around it. It's enough to make any man wish he was the object she was holding on to, which explains why she's developed such a large following in a short amount of time. Big Joe wasn't kidding when he told me she had become popular. The men here are all screaming her name. She doesn't notice, I can tell. As far as she knows at this moment, the room is empty. She's lost in the music and has tuned out all of the screaming.

I don't allow the men to touch the dancers. My girls don't dance for singles. I pay them fucking well. If the men want a lap dance, then and only then can the girls allow that. It's always in a separate room and only with a bouncer in attendance. Big Joe told me that Ana flat out refuses private dancing. I found it odd because I've checked into her pretty thoroughly. The woman is one step away from being homeless, yet she still turns down extra money. I watch as she rotates around and around the pole, defying gravity. Her spin begins to slow down and she slides to the floor, driving the men crazy. She's smiling.

There's a monitor hanging over my booth. I've never really used it since I rarely make the time to come here. Tonight, however, I am using it. I've been using it the entire time. The men are going crazy for her, salivating and dreaming of taking her home tonight. They're so lost in her body, they don't even realize that she barely notices they're there to worship her. *Ice*. It's a name that fits her. It's a name that begs an answer to the question: what could make her melt?

My eyes are continuously drawn to her hip. There's a tattoo with the word: "survivor". Just what has she survived? I wanted her from the moment I saw her, but given what's going on with her brother, I couldn't be sure what she was like in person. *Now I know*. Intriguing. I definitely want to taste her. Perhaps the most interesting thing is that I want to taste her more than once.

"What do you think, boss? I'm telling you, she doesn't mean to give you trouble. She's a good kid. I'd hate to see her get mixed up in bullshit and get hurt because her brother's a dickwad."

"Bring her to the back. Shut down any other dancers for the room until I'm finished."

"Boss, Ana doesn't do private dances."

"Don't give her a choice. I'll be waiting," I tell him, leaving without further comment.

6
Ana

"The boss is waiting for you in the backroom," Big Joe tells me just as I cinch the belt of my robe.

I look up at him as if he were insane, trying to ignore the thrill that runs through me. "Why would Yoly want me back there?" I question him, referring to the lady who hired me, even if I know better. I know who's waiting and I'm excited about it. I should be panicking.

"It's not Yoly. It's Mr. Anthes. He wants a private dance."

Electricity sizzles through me at his words. I've been thinking about Roman ever since our kiss, so much so that it worries me. I had been beating myself up ever since my last encounter with Roman. When I showed up the following day and went through my sets and Roman wasn't around, I felt a keen sense of disappointment when it should have been relief. Stupidly, I had this anticipation running through me about seeing him again. When he was nowhere to be found, it bothered me. After a few days, it became apparent that he lied. He wasn't planning on seeing me soon. I didn't play his game and he was gone. That pissed me off, even if it shouldn't. He's got my head all fucked up, and that's dangerous.

It didn't change the fact that I obsessed over it, and the more I thought about it, the more pissed I became. I'll admit that a lot of it was because he awoke things in me I have spent years trying to forget. To put it plainly, *I was horny*. It's been a long dry spell—three years, to be exact—and with one kiss, Roman brought things out in me that I'd buried deep. He succeeded so much that I've been having dreams about the man. The fact that he disappeared for two weeks and then just shows up out of the blue demanding a dance pisses me off. The bastard knows I don't do private dances. He just expects me to fall in line, like he's doing the stripper a favor and now she has to entertain him. That's the feeling that smacks me across the face and I hate it. It's a reminder of why I hate dancing.

"I don't do private dances," I insist, while in my head I'm busy trying to figure out what in the world I'm going to do. I can't risk him getting rid of me.

"You explain that to the boss. I'm just the messenger," Joe says, and it might be my imagination but I think the man is avoiding looking me in the eye. "Come on, Ana. It's not like he'll force you to do something against your will. You work for him. He's entitled to make sure you can dance."

"So he does this to all of the dancers?" I question, knowing he doesn't.

Big Joe pulls the door open and waits for me to walk past him. "You're the first dancer we've hired in a while."

I can't argue with that, but I think we both know what's going on. In fact, I think the entire room knows what is going on. It's not my imagination that the other dancers and people in the backstage area get quiet. I reach the door and glance behind me. Every dancer here who's putting on makeup or just taking a cigarette break have stopped to stare at me. The room that was crazily busy just a minute before is now deathly still and quiet.

"Hurry up, Ana. Mr. Anthes doesn't like to be kept waiting."

I pull my robe tighter around me. I'm annoyed enough that I will give him his dance, one he won't forget any time soon.

Nerves are trying to get the better of me as I stop by the small rack that contains my costumes. I grab one that makes me laugh. I think it fits Roman. Then, I grab the royal blue G-string and ignore the way it reminds me of Roman's eyes. Right now I have one goal in mind: make Roman see what he's missing and leaving him with his jaw dropped. I can do that. I mean, it's just tempting and teasing. That should be easy enough.

I waste no time getting dressed, then make my way to the private room closed off from the rest of the club. I stop at the door and inhale. Then, I push onward. My entrance is a side door that's designed for the bouncers and dancers only, completely closed off from the dancing area and surrounded by one-way glass that allows you to see into the room. *Safety*. It allows the dancers to see who they will be performing for first, a precaution that Roman himself put in when one of the girls had trouble with a crazy stalker-fan. Back when Big Joe was trying to convince me to dance, he told me everything, thinking it would make me more comfortable. It's not about the dancing, though. It's boundaries. Dancing for someone personally feels like I'm giving a piece of myself I shouldn't. This job already does that little by little. Still, Roman thinks he can take what he wants when he wants? I'll let him know that goes both ways. I thumb through the preloaded music and pick the one I want. Normally there's someone controlling the music, but Big Joe said Roman wanted privacy. *Bastard*.

The music starts pouring out of the sound system. That's my cue. *The moment of truth*. I walk out.

"You've kept me waiting, pet."

I inwardly grit my teeth and ignore him. In fact, I give him my back, trying to gather my nerves. I let my body loosen up, sinking into the music and getting lost. My hips start moving to the beat and I admit I give my ass a little extra kick when I move it in rhythm to the music, knowing it's mere inches from his face.

I can't help but wonder if he likes my costume.

7
Roman

The fucking tease!

Ana comes in the room and my dick instantly comes to life. I thought she would wear one of the sequined costumes that the dancers usually wear. Ana surprises me by wearing a school girl outfit. Long white sleeved shirt, buttoned low and revealing the valley of her breasts. The plaid mini skirt barely covers her ass. Her hair is pulled up high on her head in a ponytail and she's wearing these fake glasses. About the only diversion from the normal costume are the stiletto heels. She's so fucking hot that I want her right now. When she turns her back to me and starts dancing, rolling her ass in a slow groove, I nearly groan.

I make a living owning strip clubs. I run one of the biggest underground gambling casinos around. I have cage fighters, betting clubs, women for select clientele, and even a bail bonding business. I have my fingers in all kinds of pies and each one is different and offers something useful. It's all business. I keep it entirely separate from anything personal. That being said, not once have I ever been tempted to taste the merchandise involved in any of the businesses. *Not until Ana.* She has me breaking my own rules. And with all the women who work for me, there hasn't been one until now who can turn me on by the sway of her hips.

When she turns around, pulling one leg up high and moving it over mine so she can straddle it, it takes all of my self-control not to pounce. The reward comes when she puts both hands on my shoulders, continuing to circle her hips. She bends into my ear and says nothing, but I can feel her hot breath. *I need more.* I thought men who came here for this kind of thing were pathetic. Why waste your time on a fantasy when you could have the real thing at home?

Not only am I seeing the error in my thinking, I'm wondering just where I might play with Ana again.

Now that she's turned, her stomach is in front of me, I want to watch the way the muscles move and tighten as she grinds. I need that. "Take the shirt off, pet," I order her, my voice thick and hoarse.

She ignores me. Something she will learn in time not to do; *in time*. She does some kind of movement with her legs and easily turns back around so her ass is begging me to grab it. I manage to resist, barely. She puts both of her hands on my knee and fuck, it's the most erotic thing I've seen, the way she's moving. A man could lose himself like this. When she bends and touches the floor and her stomach and breasts graze against my leg.

She spins again, stepping between my legs this time and putting herself exactly where I want her. She places a hand on each leg, bending so her face is in front of mine. She's flushed and her violet eyes are aroused—I can see it. This dance is getting to her, too. My eyes go down to her breasts and the stiff peaks of her nipples, finding them pressed against the sheer shirt. She drops down to her knees, dancing with her whole body. My breath almost stills in my lungs as her face comes so fucking close to my crotch that I want to take over. She slithers and stretches back up, somehow getting closer. She's so close I swear I can feel her breath against my balls, even through my slacks. Ana somehow goes back, then lets her arm support her as she gyrates her ass to the floor. She sits back while extending her leg straight up, the skirt falling back and giving me a peek underneath, but not near enough. She stays leaned back, but thrusts her hips out toward me. It's a challenge to keep my face impassive. It's more than I can do to hide the giant erection currently tenting my pants.

Like a snake, she slithers back up between my legs. I watch every hypnotic roll of her body. Somehow she manages to stay in perfect time with the music. She might have not given lap dances here at the club, but she's damn perfect at them. She doesn't need to give any fucker the show I'm getting except me. *And as often as I want.* That thought only solidifies when her hands move up to the shirt and slowly starts unbuttoning. She gets two buttons undone, enough that I can see the mounds of her breasts before she turns around. She takes off the shirt with ease, but the white material blocks my view of her body. When she tosses it on the ground, I want to scream "Yes!" like a little kid.

This time after teasing me, she gives me her back, but sits down on my lap. I know she can feel my dick pressing up against her. The bastard has forgotten every hard lesson I've taught him and is practically begging. She pushes down against my dick and I know it's not my imagination that I can feel the heat from her pussy. She reaches behind her and takes my hands, sliding them up until they rest just under her breasts. She leans against me then, her arms going up and hugging around my neck. Her face is resting close enough that I can feel a gentle kiss against the pulse point of my artery. She's smiling. The tease knows she's getting to me. Then again, she'd have to be stupid to not know it. She glides back down to the floor, using it to thrust out like she might crawl. Jesus. I want her crawling to me. Would she freak out over that? I might have to train her awhile, before she would understand. She curls back around and there goes that one leg up again, giving me a glimpse of heaven. When both go up, I'm almost at my end. She hooks each leg on mine, using it to suspend her ass in the air, her body bent so much it looks like a fucking piece of erotic art. Her hands slide along her thighs and against the small covering on her pussy—silk, deep blue with small glimpses of the treasure beneath. I watch as she kicks her legs back in the air, her ass still suspended until she somehow flips over. She stands back up and this time as I watch her hips circle, she takes off her skirt a little at a time. Oddly enough, I'm glued to her face. *She's definitely smiling.*

Her breasts are jutting out, screaming her excitement. Her face is flushed, and I know if I touch her, I'll find her wet. Is it because of the dance? Would she be this way with anyone? Or is it me? It could be either—or both. Another reason her stance on no lap dances will continue.

She places those stilettos between my legs damn close to my dick. She stands up on the couch and dances like a pro before her legs bend and she comes down onto my lap. Her hands are behind my neck and she pulls my face into her breasts while her lower body grinds against my cock.

That's when my control snaps. I grab her hips and push her harder against me. She gasps as her nails dig into my head, trying to pull me deeper into her breasts. My lips seek out and find one of her breasts, and I suck the hardened nipple into my mouth.

"I don't think you're supposed to do that," she whimpers, but I notice her body is pushing harder and harder against my cock. Somehow, the bastard has moved so that she's grinding against him just right. Each movement of her hip has her sliding back and forth on my dick so that she's jacking me off in the most fucking erotic way possible.

"I'm the boss," I growl, moving from her breasts to her neck. I suck the side of her neck, loving how her pulse thrums against my tongue. I let go and find the juncture of her neck and shoulder, teasing it with my teeth. "I can do whatever the fuck I want."

"Can you make me come, before I do you? Just like this?"

she dares me.

Her question causes me to freeze as it registers, and then *I* smile. *Challenge accepted.* My mouth goes back to her breasts. I use my fingers on one and my mouth on the other to torture them both at the same time. Her thrusts against my cock quicken, her nails biting into my back so strong the pain adds to my need. My free hand that I have pulling her hip down, I move to the back of her ass. I push my fingers into that dark fold where the string of her thong rests. My fingers find the small entrance to her ass as if they were born to do that very thing. I push against it, though I never allow a finger inside.

"Oh, sweet Jesus," Ana exhales. "Roman," she whimpers and I know she's close. I can feel it from the way she's riding me.

"I'm going to win, pet," I tell her with a grin, one finger pushing into her ass so the tip of it goes in.

"If you come first, I'll lick your dick clean and drink it all down," she growls, biting into my ear. She's so far gone, I'm not sure she even realizes what she's saying. She's an animal, driven by instinct and filled with lust. That gets to me even more than her words. I thrust against her, moving both hands to her hips to command her body. I work her body against the ridge of my cock and she's helping me at the same time. I can feel my load gathering and I know I'm going to blow. I'm determined to hold back until after her, though. When she bites into my neck, hard enough that I know she's going to leave a mark, that's not possible. *She's marking me.*

I growl. My hand wraps into her hair and I take her mouth, hard. Our lips collide, our teeth and our tongues. It's all out of control, but then everything about what's going on between us right now is. I bite into her lip and notice the coppery taste of blood. I slide my tongue along it, taking that too, just as I go over the edge and come in my pants like a damn kid. My tongue is taking over her mouth and I'm going to push her over with me.

"Boss!" the banging on the door stops us both.

"Fucking hell," I mumble letting go of her mouth. "Go away!" I yell. Ana's lips spread into a smile.

"Boss! It's urgent. Bruno called!"

I stiffen, regretfully pulling Ana away from me. She whimpers, but goes.

"What's going on?" I yell again. The music in the room stops and I look down to see Ana push the button, shutting the speakers off along the back of the wall. She obviously knows the layout of the place. She's also too fucking good at lap dancing. Why does that feel like something I should make note of?

"The police raided The Stable," Joe says.

Motherfucker. I look over at Ana and watch as she buttons up the shirt she had on before. All excitement has left her eyes. Something else is there now and I have no idea what.

"This isn't finished," I warn her.

"You better go. You might want to change, though," she whispers, her face flushed and avoiding my eyes. I look down at my crotch and see a small wet circle reminding me that she made me come in my pants like a fucking kid.

"I'll have a driver waiting for you out front, Ana. He'll take you back to my place, pet, and we'll finish this," I tell her, my voice harsh because the last thing I want to do is leave her.

"You better go see to business," she says with a weak smile, though she's still not looking at me.

I grab the side of her neck and pull her to me, giving her a kiss.

"Soon, Ana. Soon," I tell her before growling my frustration out and leaving.

8
Ana

"You're late," Paul's voice says in my ear.

I pinch the bridge of my nose. It's been a rough day, I'm frustrated as hell and the last thing I need is Paul bitching at me. "Have you heard anything from Allen?"

"Nothing, Ana. I'm sorry."

"Fuck."

"How did your meeting with Roman go?"

My meeting. I don't have to have a mirror to know I'm blushing. I can feel the heat in my face. "I think I passed the test."

"Good, keep your head down and stay out of his line of sight."

Yeah, too late for that, Paul.

"Yes, daddy. Can we let it go now? We knew this was going to happen. It'll be fine. I just need you to keep looking for Allen."

"Ana, you need to prepare yourself for the—"

"Not now, Paul. I know you mean well, but right now I need to believe that Allen is alive. Until something shows me otherwise, I'm keeping with that."

"Okay, sweetheart. I'll let you know if we find anything. You checking in the same time tomorrow?"

"Yeah. I'll talk to you then."

"Stay safe," Paul says and I mumble an, "Always," as I click off my cheap burn phone. I open the drawer in my bedroom and bury it under my bras and panties, then collapse on the bed, holding my head in my hands.

I fucked up so bad today. If Paul knew what had really gone down, he'd still be ripping me a new one. How did things get so out of control? I was just going to tease him and make him loosen that tight noose of control he keeps. *Shake him up.*

I never meant to get carried away in it too.

I barely escaped going to his home tonight. That would have been a disaster. Well, it would have definitely worked out the frustration that has filled my body, but it would have been a disaster in the long run. I snuck out the back and stayed far away from the main entrance. I saw Roman's limo there waiting by the club. I wonder what his reaction will be when he realizes I'm not showing up. I was tempted, but today showed me that I'm completely out of control where Roman is concerned, and I can't afford that.

I know I only bought myself a small reprieve, but it was needed. I have to figure out what I'm going to do here. To give into my body's demands could ruin everything. Trouble is, I think I'm against the wall now and there's no other choice. None I'm willing to make right now. *None I can make.*

9
Roman

It's been a fucked up evening, leaving Ana like I did and seeing what a fucking mess the police left of my club. I'm used to mild annoyances from the police with my lesser properties, but The Stable is one of the premier spots. It's nothing to have VIP clients ranging from the hottest musicians and actors to political figures. Had this raid been on the weekend, it might have cost me plenty. As it was, I had the staff put a closed sign on the door and play it off like a fucking water leak. I paid my connections plenty to keep the story out of the press.

The cops didn't find anything. I don't think they're stupid enough to think they would, which begs the question as to what they were doing. Could Ana's questions about her brother have fallen upon the ears of a sympathetic detective trying to impress her and get in her pants? I'm going to have to quiet her down. Short of sticking my dick in her mouth, which seems like the best solution, I'm at a loss as to how.

I step out of my car, already loosening up my tie. My plan is to drink some scotch and then get lost in Ana's body. In fact, about the only bright spot of this day is Ana. Knowing she was here waiting for me kept me from going off at the club tonight.

Disappointment hits me when Ana isn't on the sofa when I enter my home. Then again, it's two in the morning. She probably gave up on me and went to bed. Which works out fine, since that's exactly where I want her. Ana and I have unfinished business, and I definitely want to finish it.

"You're home late, Mr. Anthes. Can I heat you up some dinner?" the maid Mayra asks me almost as soon as I step through the front door.

"No thanks, Mayra. I grabbed something at the club. Did you show Ana to my room?"

"Ana?"

"Didn't my driver drop off someone earlier?"

"No, sir. It's been quiet all evening."

Son of a bitch.

"Never mind, then. I must have been mistaken about the night. I'm going to crash. Goodnight."

"Goodnight sir. Try to get some rest."

I stomp into my bedroom, pissed the fuck off. I pick up the cordless phone on my nightstand and call my driver.

"I thought I told you to pick up Ana."

"Yes sir, you did. I'm still waiting at the club. She hasn't come out."

"The club closed two hours ago. There's no way she's still inside. Next time I give an order, I don't care if you have to go inside—you better make sure my orders are carried out. Do we understand each other?"

"Yes s—"

I hang up before he can finish his sentence, immediately dialing another number.

"Boss? Is something wrong?"

"I need Ana's address and phone number," I demand. "*Now.*"

"Give me a second," Joe says, sounding put-out. "Boss, she's a good kid. She's not like your usual women."

"Just get me the number, Joe." I'm not about to get into this with him. What happens with Ana is not his business. He relays the information I need and I hang up without comment, immediately dialing the number he gave me.

"Hello?" she answers, sounding surprisingly awake for the hour.

"You're not here, pet."

"Roman," she says, her voice a whispery sigh.

"Why aren't you here, Ana?"

"Roman, what happened, I... I don't think we should... It was a mistake."

"The hell it was. I'm going to send a car over."

"Roman, don't. It's late. I haven't been sleeping well and I'm dead on my feet. All I want to do is crawl in my bed and sleep."

"You can do that in my bed."

"We both know if I give in to that, we wouldn't be sleeping."

"We would eventually."

"Roman, I don't fit into your world."

"You're in my world, pet. You work in my club."

There's silence on the phone. Then she whispers one word so quiet I strain to hear it. "Temporarily."

"Ana, I don't think you understand that I'm not giving you a choice in this."

"Roman, listen to me. I know it's hard to grasp, but I'm saying no to you."

"I didn't ask."

"I noticed," she sighs. "My life is complicated right now. I have enough on my plate. I can't get mixed up in whatever trouble you have going on."

"Trouble?" I question, my body going tight.

"Police don't raid just anyone, Roman. I have a brother in trouble. He's all the anxiety I can handle right now. He's missing and I just—"

"My business is my business, Ana. Whatever happens between us, my professional life is not your concern. It does not touch you."

"You can't promise that, but it doesn't matter. I told you, I have to concentrate on finding Allen and I just don't have time in my life for a relationship."

"Again, pet, I don't do relationships *and* I'm not asking."

"Gee, Roman. You don't date, you don't do relationships …
What exactly *do* you do?"

"I'll show you. Be ready. My car will be there in fifteen."

"I can't, Roman. At least not tonight. I just got back in after
looking for my brother and I'm just too tired to move. I'm going
to nap and then head out in the morning."

Frustration runs through me at her words. Do I tell Ana and
demand she gives in to me? Do I finish off her brother and say
nothing? There are two clear paths and yet I don't take either,
mainly because I want Ana, but the first choice smacks of
desperation and that's not who I am. Ana will be mine. What
happened between us tonight did nothing but chisel that in stone.

"I'm sending my car over. You can sleep here and sleep in."

"Roman, I can't. My—"

"I will help you find your brother, Ana. Now get enough stuff
together for a couple of days and I'll have my driver pick you up
in twenty minutes."

"You'll help me find Allen?" she asks, her voice full of
disbelief.

She could join the crowd. The minute I said the words, I
wanted them back. It's too late and what's done is done. I have
no fucking idea what I'm doing other than getting Ana in my
bed. That seems to be the only important thing right now.

"I don't know the particulars," I tell her, lying, "but
tomorrow we'll talk and I'll help you. I'm sure my contacts are
better than yours."

"Roman," she whispers, her voice breaking.

"Twenty minutes, Ana."

"I'll be ready."

"Good. See you soon," I tell her before clicking the phone off and calling my driver and giving him Ana's address. I go to the bar and poor myself a drink while undoing my cufflinks and putting them down. I take off the tie completely and unbutton my shirt, leaving it on. I collapse in the chair facing the bed, drink in hand.

Chasing a woman. What the hell is wrong with me? I hope I know what the fuck I'm doing.

10
Ana

Paul is going to kill me. Hell, I might even kill me if Roman doesn't beat us both to the punch. I can't believe I'm doing this. I couldn't resist though. When Roman said he would help me find Allen, I had to give in. I'd like to play the martyr and say that's the only reason I gave in, but it would be a lie. I wanted to see Roman again. I wanted to have this time with him. It has nothing to do with my brother. Jesus, maybe being fucked up runs in my family. I thought I might have been the one sane one, but signs are starting to point to the fact that I'm as screwed up, if not more, as my mother and Allen combined.

I spend the next fifteen minutes throwing a few things in an overnight bag and mentally berating myself. The longer I think about what I just agreed to, the more my nerves close in around me. When someone starts knocking on my door, I nearly jump out of my skin. I pull the strap of my satchel over a shoulder and walk to the door, cursing myself silently in my head.

"Who is it?"

"I'm Mr. Anthes's driver. He said you would be expecting me."

"I'm ready," I tell him, opening the door. I'm also lying through my teeth. He's a tall man, maybe about the size of Roman, but he definitely lacks his presence. He's wearing a black suit and keeps his hand on my back the entire walk outside. He takes me to a large, black, stretch limousine.

As we approach, he opens the car door. "Ms. Stevens, there's a minibar and television in the back." His words go through me. I feel like Alice and I've stepped through some kind of rabbit hole.

The door closes and I settle inside, the leather interior feeling softer than I remember leather being before. I keep my hands in my lap, afraid to touch anything. The limo starts up, the engine running so quietly that had there not been a change in the vibration of the air around me, I'm not sure I would have noticed. The darkened partition between the front seat and the back slowly slides down.

"We'll be there in about forty minutes, Ms. Stevens. If you need anything, there's an intercom button on your door."

My eyes seek out the button and find it. I turn back to the driver.

"Um. Couldn't we just communicate like this?"

"Most of Mr. Anthes's passengers like privacy."

The small fine hairs on the back of my neck tingle at the chauffeur's words. Why does it feel like by "passengers" he means "women"? That's basically what I am, right? A woman he's pursing for sex. I'm old enough and lived through enough that if I want a quick fling with a man—or hell, even a one-night-stand—I should feel no shame. The problem is that Roman is the last man on earth I should pick to do that with. Things are complicated and this is just going to make it more so.

"I'm not like his normal passengers," I tell the driver, because if nothing else, I am completely sure of that. "What's your name?' I ask him, needing the idle conversation to still my nerves.

"Robert."

"Hi Robert, I'm Ana."

"Hi, Ana," he says and smiles at me through the rearview mirror.

"Where are we going exactly?" I ask, because I have no idea.

"Mr. Anthes lives on the east side of the city. We'll be there in no time."

The rest of our ride is relatively quiet and full of passing small talk about the weather and the NBA playoffs, of which I know next to nothing. I figure men and sports go together easily enough, so I fake my way through the conversation. He takes me further out onto a dirt road. I didn't know there was a place this remote in all of Miami. My survival instincts have kicked in and I feel nerves skitter down my back. Did my conversation with Roman about my brother trigger something for him? I clutch my satchel close to me.

"I thought Mr. Anthes lived in an apartment near his nightclub?" I ask Robert just as we're rounding a curve. My tight hold on my satchel loosens as a large iron gate with a big "A" on it comes into view. You can see a paved road from that point on and it leads to a gigantic mansion beside the ocean. *Hello, world. Meet money.*

"He owns a hotel there and keeps the top floor to stay in, but this is his house."

"Oh. Does he bring many people out here?"

Silence. Guess I asked too many questions.

When the car comes to a stop, I spend a few seconds to catch my breath when Robert gets out of the car. I turn when the door opens, but it's not Robert standing there; it's Roman. His hair is disheveled, he's got a five o'clock shadow going, and his shirt is completely unbuttoned which leaves a line of bronze perfection to draw my eye. Instantly, I wish the shirt was gone—and then I want to slap the stupid out of me.

Roman reaches his hand in. I stare at it for a minute before putting mine in his. White hot heat runs through my system. Never has this happened to me before, this instant electric connection to someone that is so powerful, it short-circuits my brain cells. Why does the one man it happens with have to be Roman Anthes?

He helps me out, but my legs feel like jelly. I nearly fall and stumble against him. I brace myself on his chest, my fingertips burning when they touch his bare skin. His arms go around me and I get lost in the musky smell of his aftershave and the scent that is just him. *Strong. Powerful. Alpha.*

"That will be all for today, Robert. Put Ms. Steven's bag inside the house," Roman tells the driver, as if bringing a woman to his house at almost three a.m. is an everyday occurrence.

"Very well, sir." Robert says. I hear him, but my eyes are glued to Roman's face and the look in his eye as he watches me.

"You dance in these shoes. Is there some reason you're having trouble walking in them?" Roman asks, his arms still around me.

"Gee. I'm going to go with nerves. My boss at work is trying to tie me in knots," I snap.

"I do plan on tying you up, pet, but I'll make sure you like it," he says with a dark smile.

I think my ovaries just spontaneously combusted. I really need to get a handle on things.

I swallow at his words and ignore the shudder of excitement that runs through me. "Roman, I told you this is just not a good idea. I came here to get your help to find my brother. I'm just not looking for a relationship right now."

"Neither am I."

"Then why are you doing this?"

"I don't do relationships, pet. I want to fuck you."

His words steal my breath. How do I respond? I should slap his face. I shouldn't be interested in this man, but there's some type of pure male magnetism surrounding him, and I'd be lying if I didn't admit that from the moment I first saw him, I wanted him. That's what dancing for him was all about. It was reckless and stupid, but then being here is, too.

"I don't do one-night-stands, and could you please quit calling me that? I'm not a dog."

His deep brown eyes flick over my body.

"Perhaps I didn't make myself clear, Ana. You don't have a choice in this," he says.

"What are you doing?" I cry, beating against his chest when he pulls me up in his arms, carrying me toward the front door of his home.

He grabs both of my hands in one of his, securing it around my wrists. He leans down so that our lips are just a breath apart. The heat coming off of him surrounds me and robs me of my voice.

"This will not be a one-night-stand, *pet*." His dark voice slithers over me and I'm frozen, unable to move, glued to the promise written all over his face. "This will be about submission. *Yours*. You will give yourself to me in every way you can possibly imagine."

"You're crazy," I whisper. I deny him, but I'm afraid because I can hear the surety in his voice and I'm called to it.

"On the contrary, I'm quite sane. Give me your lips, Ana."

"This is crazy. Why would I submit to you?"

"Because I will give you more pleasure than your body could ever imagine."

"Roman," I start, but he doesn't let me finish.

"And because, Ana, you won't have a choice. Now, give me your lips."

I pull against his hold, needing to get away from him, to breathe, to try and think, because I'm being drugged by the scent of him, by the feel of him surrounding me, by the need in his voice and the dark promises in his eyes. All of it is closing in on me and seducing me.

The harder I pull, the rougher his hold becomes on my hip

until his fingers are biting into my skin. I gasp at the sting of pain and the rough way he handles me.

"We can do this the easy way or the hard way, pet. I prefer the easy right now. But, I will not lie to you. I will be a happy man if you choose the hard way. I will enjoy the fuck out of going that route with you. So, choose Ana."

"I don't understand," I tell him, thoroughly confused. Perhaps it is my lack of sleep, or stress has taken its toll on me and I have completely lost it. Whatever it is, I am completely out of my depth for the first time in my life.

"Give. Me. Your. Lips." His order comes off as dark words punctuated with heavy need. There's no way I should obey his command. No way on earth. Yet, my head bends into him, wanting his kiss, *craving* it.

He takes my lips, claiming them with a fierceness that should terrify me, but instead sets my body aflame. He sucks my tongue into his mouth, torturing and teasing it with his own. He plunders every corner of my mouth, every small nook and crevice, and his taste is a mixture of alcohol, lust, and all man.

The kiss changes slowly. It becomes more about calming and enjoying instead of possessing, and only then do I break away to drag oxygen into my lungs. My breathing is heavy, my heart hammers against my chest, and my body hums with pleasure. I can feel his cock pushing into my hip and he's rock hard. The heat from it alone brands me. I bite my lip to keep from rubbing against it like a cat in heat.

Roman stares at me for another moment, then brings my wrists up to his mouth and kisses the inside of each one before letting them go. I feel one of his hands petting my hair and a second later, his voice is at my ear. "Very good, pet. You just earned one reward."

I have no idea what that means. I just remain silent. Words

are beyond me right now. I never knew kisses like that existed and the fact that I just shared one with Roman is yet another reason to be terrified of what I'm doing. *Paul is going to kill me.*

11

Roman

I take Ana into my house and sit on the sofa with her. I keep her in my lap. My hands pet her hair and her arms, getting her used to my touch, training her to need it. She doesn't try to get off my lap, but she starts looking around the room. I watch her face as she takes it all in, wanting to judge her reaction. She doesn't know it, but she's the first woman besides my employees that I've allowed through the doors. Then again, something tells me that Ana will be special, otherwise I wouldn't be pursuing her this hard.

"Do you like it?" I ask, looking around the room and trying to see it from her eyes. I never thought about it really. I hired Miami's premiere design company to decorate. There's a lot of white with large splashes of turquoise and orange and lime greens, all colors associated with the beach and life in Miami, or so my decorator said—something about the colors being warm and vibrant. To be honest I never really cared. Now I wonder if it falls short in Ana's eyes. I'd like to know her thoughts.

"It's nice."

That's it. I may have not had other women here, but instinctively I know they would have noticed the designer's handiwork. They would have seen the top-of-the-line furnishings and expensive paintings and had dollar signs in their eyes. Ana's eyes are not like that. In fact, I get the feeling she doesn't like the house at all and is trying to be *nice*. I don't normally smile, but that thought has me doing so now. I have to wonder if this is the first of Ana's surprises for the night.

I stand up and slowly let her go to the floor. She takes a

breath as her feet hit the floor, but I still keep her wrapped up in my arms, not wanting to let her go completely yet. Her hands brace on my shoulders as she takes off her high heels. I'm not sure what she thinks she would hurt or why she's bothering. I've never met a woman who has taken her shoes off unless they were stripping for me and a lot of those times they leave their shoes on. Being barefoot obviously feels better. Does she feel that comfortable with me? I make note to have thick carpet installed if this works out. That way, her feet can stay warm.

I lead her down the hall towards the master bedroom. I keep it on the main floor and reserve the upstairs for guest rooms, which are never used. I don't want guests. *Ever*. Ana is the only one I will break that rule for.

Ana freezes at the entrance. Inside is a large king-size four-poster bed, a large television hanging on the wall and a low line sleek black dresser with matching nightstands. It has a sitting area off to the left of the bed and then behind that is an open master bath with a sunken tub and large steam shower.

"A problem, Pet?"

"Is … Is this the bedroom you want me to stay in?" she says, trying to back away.

"This is my bedroom."

"I'll just wait for you outside then. Or you could tell me where your guest room is."

"You'll be staying here with me, Ana."

"I don't think so."

I ignore her comment and apply more pressure at her back to get her moving. Her eyes are focused on the bed. I wonder if, like me, she is imagining being tied to it later. I'm biding my time until I can do that very thing. There's never been a woman in this bed. I've never wanted one. But I'm making another exception and it's for the same reason. *Ana*.

44

"Have you eaten?" I ask her, pulling my shirt off.

"What? Umm ... no, I guess I haven't."

"Good. I'll have the cook heat up dinner for us."

"You do realize it's three a.m.," she says, as I pick up the phone and inform the kitchen staff what I want.

"I don't keep regular hours, Ana. I pay my staff enough to reflect that and reward them for understanding. I'm going to take a shower while dinner is getting heated. I'll just be a few minutes. Unless you'd like to join me?" I ask her, putting my shirt on the bed.

"Join you?" she parrots, sitting in the chair that I keep in front of the bed. *Disappointing.* I would much rather have her on the bed waiting for me.

"In the shower."

"I, uh ... I think I will be fine here," she says.

"A pity." I like the way her eyes are drawn to my chest almost as much as I like the way the heat rises into her face.

"Listen, Roman, I'm not sure what your game is, but I think it would be best if I leave. I'm not—" Ana starts, heading to the door and showing more fire in this moment than she has since I've started toying with her.

"Not what, Ana?" I ask, taking a step and catching her easily. My hand encircles her waist, making sure she doesn't get away.

"I'm not your plaything. Your *pet.* I don't understand what is going on between us or what you think tonight is about. I wanted your help to find my brother. Clearly we are not on the same page. I just think it would be best if we ended it here and I get back to my world and you can find someone else to follow you around like a puppy and obey," she says.

She gets it all out in one large breath, which is also commendable. The heat is blaring across her face, her blush so dark she glows. I commend her on showing backbone. I'm much too used to women following my commands.

My thumb brushes against the pulse point in her wrist, enjoying the erratic beat. More to the point, enjoying how I can see the outline of her nipples against her t-shirt and the way her chest rises and falls as if she's been running. "Do I affect you, Ana?"

"Affect me?" she whispers, and I watch as her throat works when she swallows.

"Is there a part of you that wants to join me in the shower? To help me take my clothes off and finish what we started when you danced for me? Are you thinking about what it would feel like to give me your body under the hot spray of the water? To feel my hands on you, or my lips? Do you secretly want to give in to that naughty side of yourself and see if the promise in my words would be as good as it sounds?"

Her gasp echoes in the room, but it's the way it leaves her mouth open that I respond to. I keep my hold on her wrist tight, using it to pull her even closer to me, and then I kiss her for the second time tonight, claiming her lips with a hunger and a need that I didn't experience before Ana. This time, there's no wait as her tongue instantly joins mine, warring with it and trying to come out victorious. I let out a deep guttural growl, feral almost. Definitely animal-like, because that's what Ana reduces me to. Her sweet taste intoxicates me as our tongues rap around each other, fighting for dominance, and then we break apart to stare into each other's eyes. I may have won the battle, but I'm almost definite that she has captured me in some type of trap.

Ultimately, I don't think I care as long as I end up between her legs.

12
Roman

I watch as Ana's fingers go to her bruised lips, touching them and feeling the damage I left behind. I wasn't gentle. I never intend to be.

"We shouldn't have done that," she whispers, but those violet eyes of hers are shining.

"Done what?"

"The dance. It shouldn't have happened. Just like that kiss shouldn't have happened. This is wrong, Roman."

"Don't bother saving face. Before the night is through, we'll be doing a lot more."

"I don't think you understand. I'm here because of my brother. I don't just jump into men's beds. I may take my clothes off for strangers in your club, but that doesn't mean I do the same in private. I reserve that for a man I know, a man I like, a man I'm dating."

"You like me."

"We're not dating. I don't think you get what a date even is."

"I get that it's for people who are too backwards to admit what they want from each other," I tell her, advancing on her until she backs into the side of the bed. I move so she falls back on it and then I pin her to it with the weight of my body. I grab each of her wrists and hold them above her head, making her completely helpless. Instead of screaming at me, she cries out and then bites her lip, studying my face. "I'm going to tell you exactly what I want from you, Ana. I want your body. Willingly offered to me anytime and anyway I want it. I want you submitting to me. I want your trust that no matter what I ask, you'll do it, because you know that when it comes down to it, you will love where I take you. I want—"

"Complete control," she whispers, interrupting me.

I smile. She gets it, and while she's tense beneath me, she's not trying to leave. I've made a fortune out of reading faces and, unless I'm totally missing something, she's more than interested.

"Complete control," I confirm.

"I'm not sure I'm cut out for this."

"How about we try it out for one night and see."

"Why me?"

"Because it's you I want. And when I want something, I don't stop until I get it. It's as simple as that, Ana."

Her head comes up off the mattress and she presses her lips gently to my mouth. Her sweet little tongue comes out to lick mine. Her eyes are wide open as she whispers.

"Do I get a safe word?" she asks.

I'm intrigued. Has she been in this type of relationship before, or does she just know things from reading or watching movies?

"You won't need one tonight, pet. But yes, you will get one if this works out." It's a small lie. There's no if; this *is* working out. I'm keeping her—at least until I grow bored. I have a feeling that Ana will hold my interest longer than any woman before her.

"Show me."

Surprise. Green light. I wasn't expecting it. I truthfully thought I would have to work for it harder. I'm a sadistic bastard and I can admit there's a part of me that's disappointed I'm not going to have to work for her. The part that controls my dick tells the rest of me to shut the fuck up.

"I plan on it," I tell her, taking the kiss she offers.

13
Ana

I've lost my mind. I know I have. That's the only explanation. I knew coming here tonight was a risk and I was insane to even think about it, but I thought I could control it— keep ahead of Roman and direct how tonight went. *Maybe.* Maybe I'm just lying to myself. Maybe I still am. Roman doesn't know my real life. He has no idea who I am and the kind of person I am. My life is so swamped with responsibility, stress, and trying to take care of everyone. Roman is forbidden. Forbidden in ways that should scare the hell out of me and keep me from doing this. It doesn't. He calls to me, and the lure of giving him complete control is too much to turn down. There's this little voice inside that tells me I can keep up this image that Roman sees and use it to my advantage. I'll enjoy a taste of the freedom he's offering while getting behind his defenses. Getting closer to use him to find my brother sounds cold, but most of life is, and Roman Anthes is as coldhearted as they come. If he finds out, he'll kill me, but he doesn't have to find out; I just have to be careful.

All thought of bargaining or justifying goes out the window when he kisses me. His tongue pushes into my mouth and, just like before, it warms me instantly. I pull against his hold, wanting to touch him. His hold doesn't budge. *Complete control.* I remind myself and I let go of everything and just feel. His kiss is slower this time, searching and conquering me. He pulls away slowly, standing up over me. My hands are free now, but for the life of me I can't bring them down. I'm hypnotized by the look on his face.

He kicks his shoes off and somehow he manages to make that sexy. My body feels like it's on fire. I'm struggling to force air out of my lungs and the exertion makes my body shudder with each ragged exhale. When his hands come to his belt and he begins undoing it, I forget to breathe altogether. I watch as the shiny black belt slides away from his pants. He gathers it in one hand before coming back on the bed overtop of me. He's so much larger than me, and this time when he blankets me, it's his chest over my face. I can't resist placing kisses along the top of his abs and then further up the middle of his chest. His skin has a taste that goes straight to my head. Man and sex; if those were flavors, they'd be his. I finally remember I have arms again and can't wait to touch him, to learn every contour of his body, to dig my nails into his back as he's pounding me.

Before I can, he has my wrists again and he cinches them together in his belt. The action causes my heart to speed up, but it's not from fear. *Complete control*, I hear his voice whisper in my mind. Need thrums through my blood quickly. I want this. How he knew what I craved is beyond me. It may be wrong, but I'm going to let go and gain enough memories to last me a lifetime. I pull against the belt, but it doesn't budge. I don't question him. I instinctively know this would be wrong. I don't want to do anything that might stop him at this point.

I look over my head as best as I can to watch him secure the belt against the headboard. When he's done, my hands are locked in place and there's not a thing I can do to move them. *Complete control,* I hear again in my head, and along with arousal this time there is a trace of nerves. Reality tries to interfere as I watch him walk slowly and purposely to the foot of the bed and directly into my sight. He wants me to see him. He's getting off on me being helpless. While I have to admit I am, I don't know this man besides what I've read and our limited interaction. What if he goes too far? *What was I thinking?* I start to tell him I've changed my mind when he distracts me. His hand goes to the button of his slacks. My eyes zero in on the movement and it's almost as if everything is in slow motion as he unfastens it. Then, I watch as even slower his hand moves the zipper down. As his pants fall to the floor, his cock springs out, definitely ready to play, and I nearly lose it.

"My God," I whisper before I can stop myself. So much for playing it cool. Until this moment, I thought I could play cool with the best of them. It's the only way I've survived in my line of work; I've perfected it down to a science. All signs of being cool are gone now, blown completely to smithereens, and I can do nothing but stare at the massive cock between his legs. It's at least ten inches, maybe longer, but that's not what scares me. *It's wide.* I don't think there's any way possible one of my hands could encircle it.

Roman laughs. "See something you like, pet?"

I lick my lips because they are so parched it feels as if I've not had anything to drink in months. Ever since the dance earlier today, I've been on edge. No. Let's call a spade a spade. *I'm horny.* I have never been horny in my life. It's another reason I can be so calm and cool. My life is chaos and there's no time for personal needs. The few men I've been with have been pleasant, even good, but nothing I missed when I crawled in bed by myself at night.

"You'll split me apart," I tell him because apparently being horny means your filters are gone and you blurt things out without thinking.

Roman, for his part, throws his head back in the first show of full-fledged laughter that I've seen. Like this, he's sexier. His body is relaxed and he doesn't seem as distant or unreachable. Of course, it could be because with each movement of his body, his cock dances against him, tempting me even further.

"Not hardly, pet. But for now, that doesn't matter."

"It doesn't?" I ask, watching as a thin line of clear liquid runs from the dark head of his cock and along the shaft, painting one of the large veins that bulges against the skin. My tongue comes out, wanting to taste it, to bring it into my mouth and drink it.

"No, you're not getting my cock right now." Angels are probably crying in heaven. I can hear them and I join them with my protesting whimper. "Shh, pet. You will get it … in due time. When you've earned it. For now I have a different game in mind."

When I've earned it? Everything in me protests, but I shut it down. *Complete control.*

"What game?" I ask, unable to move my eyes from his cock. It's hypnotizing me, the way it's moving back and forth, taunting me with its size.

"Do you know what one of my favorite things is, Ana?"

"What?" I ask, wondering how he expects me to carry on a coherent conversation like this.

"Watching a woman completely lost in her orgasm. Watching every moment as it comes crashing down on her and seeing the exact moment that she loses touch with reality and finally lets go."

Those words bring my eyes back to him. Perhaps I should have done that sooner, because he has something in his hand. It's glittery and purple and has these thin straps attached to it.

"What is that?"

"Something that will make you feel really good, sweet, sweet Ana," he says softly, putting a knee on the bed. I watch as he attaches one of the straps around my waist. His hand moves down to caress my pussy. "I love that you are bare and so beautiful. Such a delicate pink. I'm going to take real good care of this pussy, pet." He forgot the word "wet" because I'm definitely that, and at his words, I just get wetter. There's no time to be embarrassed because Roman's finger slides between the lips and strokes against my swollen clit. My hips jerk off the bed, my hands pulling against the restraint without success.

"Yes, please," I moan as he glides over it again. My body feels as if it is on fire. I don't think it will take much to set me off. I jerk though when I feel the cold silicone slide against my pussy and push up against my clit, stretching it into place. "What's that?"

"This is called a butterfly, sweet Ana. Have you ever played with one before?"

I try to concentrate on his words and on the excitement I felt earlier and stop the panic inside of me. "What?" I gasp, but he stills my protest with a gentle kiss against my stomach. It's tender and sweet and completely different from what is going on between us.

He leaves the bed and I notice a chair behind where he was standing before. I was so engrossed in him, I didn't notice it earlier. I do now because he sits in it, naked as the day he was born, though obviously there's a lot more to him now. He seems like this is just another day for him. Maybe it is. Right now, he appears to not have a care in the world, as if he doesn't have me tied to the bed—

All thoughts end as I feel a soft vibration begin fluttering against my pussy. It's soft, barely more than a ghost touch, *a tease*, just enough to get my attention. I swallow hard, my body heated and my breath short. The blood is thrumming through my veins and echoing so loud in my ears that I'm sure Roman can hear it. He shows no sign of it. He sits there in silence. In fact, the only sound in the room is my ragged breathing and the quiet hum of the vibrator. I can do nothing but watch him. Time has ceased to have meaning. I know it's been awhile. Twenty minutes? *Thirty?* It could have been even more and nothing new happens. *Except...*

The small stimulation is starting to get to me. I can feel the changes in my body: the tightening in my breasts, the creamy wetness I can feel dripping from my pussy ... it all slowly directs me to an edge I know I will eventually fall over. There's nothing I can do to stop it—or to come. I would definitely take that choice. My hands pull against the bindings, but it doesn't let me move. With each passing moment, my need increases. My body twists and turns, trying to find what it needs, but nothing I'm doing helps.

"Roman, please," I whimper, needing more.

"Very good, pet. You just earned a reward."

Reward? Why does he keep saying that?

My brain is hazy, the needs of my body and its demands taking over. I try to make sense out of what he is saying, but can't. It becomes crystal clear however just a minute later. The vibrator shifts speeds and moves faster. Its pulsations rake through my body.

"Oh, God," I whine. My body feels as if there's a fire running through it, burning me from the inside out.

"No, pet. Roman, not *God.*"

His gravelly voice hits me and my insides flutter even more. He could own my soul with that voice. *Not God?* Maybe he's not. Maybe he's the Devil himself, a beautiful lost angel sent down to destroy my soul.

14
Ana

"Beg me, pet. Ask me for what you want," he continues.

I stretch my body, my back curving as I moan out his name. Feeling nothing but pleasure as the vibration hits exactly on my clit and around it all at the same time. It feels as if he's delivering soft kisses over and over against the most sensitive part of me. I imagine it's Roman's tongue teasing my clit over and over. I squeeze my legs together as I feel my climax begin to build. I give in and give him exactly what he wants.

"Roman, please. *More.* I need more," I tell him, my eyes connecting with his. I'm completely at his mercy. He's watching everything I do. I see a trace of a smile on his lips. It's beautiful, but it's his hands that my vision is drawn to. He's working his cock. His hand is sliding back and forth on his shaft. It's glistening and slick with his pre-cum. He stands up, revealing his other hand, the one holding the remote. He flicks his thumb and instantly I feel the vibrations from the toy increase. My body bows in half as my legs come onto the mattress. I push my lower body up in the air, looking for more. Needing more of whatever I can find, but finding nothing. Visions of his cock thrusting inside of me, widening and stretching me and owning my body, instantly come to mind. I picture his cock pounding harder and harder deep inside of me. Just those thoughts are enough to bring me to my limit.

"Roman! I'm going to come!"

"Not yet, pet. You can't come until I tell you to."

I do my best to focus on him. *He can't be serious.*

"Roman, I can't."

"Not until I tell you, pet. Your pleasure is mine," he instructs.

"I can't wait, Roman. I have to…"

I break off my words when he turns the vibrator off completely. I cry out in frustration. The disappointment is so severe that tears sting my eyes. I want to curse him, to scream and throw things. But then *I can't*. He asked for this. *Complete control.*

"Please, Roman. Make me come," I beg him. "Please," I add, so there can be no doubt how desperate I am, or that I doubt he is in charge.

That seems to satisfy him because he turns the vibrator back on. I moan and literally weep in relief. Instantly the orgasm starts building again. I tap down my desire. I don't want to make Roman unhappy again. I need everything he is giving me.

"Can I come, Roman? Please? It's… I'm so close. I need to come." I'm not sure what I'm telling him at this point. I just know I'm begging and needing his approval. I didn't even realize my eyes were closed until I feel his hand on my stomach. I look at him as he flips the switch on the remote again. My breath stalls, wondering exactly what will happen. The speed is the same, though the vibrations are deeper. There's a pulsing beat added into the mix now. I feel heat flush through my body. I know I'm gone now. There's no way I can hold back any longer. "Roman," I plead.

"Come, pet. Come for me," he tells me.

I detonate as my climax rockets through me, crashing down on me in wave after heavy wave. I ride it out, my body on an overload of pleasure, and the source is all coming from Roman. Just when I'm about to calm down, he must hit another button on the control. I can't even describe what it does. It feels as if a hundred and one fingers are manipulating my clit at once. I go over the edge again, screaming Roman's name. His large hand rubs against my stomach, caressing me. My eyes search him out again. He's out of focus because I think most of my body is floating somewhere in another universe, but I see him. He's stroking his cock. Streams of pre-cum drip off of his shaft, covering his hand and then dripping down onto my skin. I moan as aftershocks of my latest orgasm shake my body. That's when I feel the first heated splash of his cum coat my stomach as he comes with me. *On me.*

"Something wrong, pet?" I ask Ana as we sit at the table.

After our first little playtime, we showered together. I washed her hair and her body, making sure to get her pussy off with my fingers. I wanted to fuck her right there, but part of the fun in breaking in a new toy is taking your time and enjoying the slow ride until they wonder if you will ever give them what they really want. Ana is a bit different, though. I'm having to fight myself to hold back, and that's never happened before. *How many times has this woman surprised me?* I'm losing count. I've never had that in my life. I've always known how people will react. It's what has made me successful over the years.

This woman surprises me every time I turn around.

"I could probably eat better in my own chair," she says, a fine pink tint spreading on her face. How she can blush after the way she just came, is yet another surprise. She doesn't hide her reactions to me. She doesn't have a mercenary bone in her body that I can find. It's refreshing.

She's in my lap, and we're sitting at the dining room table waiting while my cook heats up the spaghetti and bolognaise sauce. I put a white silk robe on her and brushed her hair and she looks even younger than she did before. If I hadn't read her file I'd have to ask her if she was legal. She sure as hell doesn't look twenty-seven.

"There's no need. I'm going to feed you."

"You're going to feed me?" she asks, her face registering her shock.

"Complete control tonight. Remember?"

She still feels tense in my hands, but she relaxes a little more. Mayra, my maid, brings water, a plate of food, and a basket of bread.

"Thank you," Ana says, but Mayra doesn't acknowledge her, which makes the blush on Ana's face darken. I may have to have a talk with my staff. I immediately dismiss the idea. I will be putting Ana up in her own apartment. The point is moot.

I wrap some of the spaghetti around my fork and bring it to her mouth. She opens, sucking the noodles inside her mouth. "That's good," she says.

"My chef is good. I demand the best from the people around me," I tell her, feeding her again.

"I'm picking up on that. What happens when something is beyond your control?" she asks, her hand coming up to catch some of the sauce which has been caught on her lip.

"That rarely happens. I told you I like—"

"Complete control. Yeah, I kind of got that from what happened in the bedroom and shower."

I pull her hand to my mouth and suck off the remnants of the sauce she has there, letting my tongue glide around her finger before releasing it.

"Exactly."

"Am I going to be calling you Daddy before the night is over?" she asks, reaching over and pulling out some of the noodles with her fingers. Her head goes back to let the noodles slink into her opened mouth. My cock pushes up against her ass. I should reprimand her for feeding herself, but since it's the hottest fucking thing I've seen and my eyes are still glued to the way she's sucking the red meat sauce off her fingers, I don't.

"Some have. Others, no. That is completely your choice, as long as you give me what I want," I reply, watching her feed herself again.

This time she stops before swallowing the spaghetti down to look at me. "Then no thank you. I had one Daddy. He wasn't that great. And please, can we not refer to your other *pets*? I don't want to lose my appetite."

"Jealous?"

"Just trying to forget the fact that I'm just one in a succession of women for you."

I let that remark slide because she's not wrong, even if discussing this with her feels wrong.

"Tell me about your *daddy*."

"I'd rather not. That's another subject that will make me lose my appetite."

"Is that so?" I ask her, suddenly envious of spaghetti.

She sucking more of them down her mouth and, at my words, she stops when the last of them disappear into her mouth. I grab the noodles this time, holding them over her lips. I hold them a little high so I can watch while her delicate neck stretches up. She sucks them into her mouth slowly, her eyes on me the entire time. She's deliberately trying to turn me on, even while she's blushing wildly. The combination is sexy as hell.

"Not like you. I mean, I was talking like a father, but he doesn't really qualify for that either. He gives the term 'dead-beat-dad' a new meaning."

"I see. And your mother?" I ask her, already knowing the answer but enjoying the way she's opening up so frankly to me. No games. No hidden meanings. Ana doesn't do mysterious or coy and I like it. She's also not trying to buy me with sympathy. Too many women have tried to make me their meal ticket by giving me sob stories. It never seemed to matter that I didn't really care what their stories were. Ana might be different in that respect too—yet another surprise.

"She split before my father did. Though she did make

appearances here and there, mostly when she needed money. I won the lottery in the parental department," she says, reaching around for the bread. She grabs a piece, but before she can do anything with it, I take it away. She starts to protest, but I pinch a corner off of it and pop it into her waiting mouth, letting my finger slide over her bottom lip, the butter from the bread makes the touch on her lips smooth.

"Who raised you?"

"My father didn't go MIA until I was sixteen." She shrugs, leaving me to fill in the blanks. *Which I do.*

"Was it just you and your brother?" I prod, wondering exactly what she will say.

"Yeah. Drink, please?" she asks this time, instead of getting it herself. I get the water and guide it to her lips. She scrunches up her face but takes a drink.

"I'm not really a water drinker," she says.

"It's good for you."

"So's spinach. I find I don't like it, either," she says, her nose curling.

"But water is very useful." I put the glass down on the table.

"To grow spinach?"

"To make you *wet*," I tell her, shifting her body so that she has a leg on either side of me now and her back is against the table.

"I know of other things that do that," she whispers, biting on the corner of her mouth again, which I've come to realize is a nervous gesture of hers.

I reach into the glass with one hand capturing a piece of the ice. I flick the sash to her robe loose, revealing one of her breasts. I put the cube into my mouth sucking it in and then letting the tip out. I lower my lips to her, letting the ice hover there. She sucks the tip, her eyes open.

"Roman," she whispers brokenly, her voice laced with hunger. I lean down so I can rake the ice down her chin, following an imaginary line down her beautiful neck. An immense feeling of satisfaction comes over me when I see the trail of wetness I leave in my wake. Her head is back, allowing me access, and after a couple of passes down her neck, I move to her breast. I circle the outside. Ana really has gorgeous breasts. They're big, but not obscenely so. I can cover them with my hand and they are full, soft, and pliable. Perfect, really. I move the ice around her areola. Her nipple, which was already hard, is pebbled so tightly it looks painful. The ice is almost gone, so I move to her other nipple, letting the icy water drip down. It's stunning to watch the way the water drips and runs around the nipple and then along the fine ridges that have been made on her areola because of her excitement. I watch until I can't anymore, and then I take the nipple in my mouth, my tongue swirling the last remnants of the ice around, and I suck it so hard it may bruise. A combination of the cold and my mouth makes Ana cry out. Her hands go to my head and she tries to drag me into her. When I finish, I pull away to look at the stormy violet depths staring back at me. They're full of hunger and need.

"Your dinner is getting cold, pet," I remind her, doing my best not to grind against her body. My cock is as hard as brick, pushing up against her bare pussy. The sweatpants I pulled on do nothing to block out the feel of her.

"I'm not hungry for food," she whispers.

My hands flex into her hips, biting into them, and even the sting of that doesn't bother her. I pull her roughly to the side, using my hand to swipe the dishes from the table. They fall to the pristine granite floor in a heap of broken glass, porcelain dishes, and food.

"What are you—" Ana rasps, grabbing my shoulders tight as

I stand up, placing her on the table.

"Having my dinner. I'm starved," I growl, putting pressure on her chest so she falls gently back, flat against the table.

16

Roman

"Roman, the mess—your maid," Ana whispers, but I ignore her. My fingers bite into her ass as I pull her into me.

"Fuck the mess, pet," I tell her, just before my tongue pushes between the lips of her pussy and her taste fills my mouth. What is it about her? What is it that makes this woman irresistible? When I was younger, women were a must. For a while now though, building my business and making my name took precedence. I've had a few partners. Handpicked, backgrounds checked, and contracts signed. Sex is a business just like every other thing in my life.

Until now. I've broken every rule I've ever had with Ana. She'll definitely be mixing business with pleasure, considering I'll most likely kill her brother.

There's no contract in place, which is a major concession. And here I am, a grown man of forty-two, diving into the pussy of a woman I haven't had medically examined. That should be enough to cool me off and make me pull back. The fact that it's not is worrisome, but right now I couldn't care less.

"Roman," she breathes.

If you can get addicted to the way someone says your name, then I am definitely there. I flatten my tongue and slide it through her cream until I hit her swollen clit. I suck the nub into my mouth, using the pressure and my teeth to tease and torment it. Her hands reach for my head and I pull up.

"Keep your hands down, Ana. I'll give you everything you need."

Her body jerks in response and her hands slam down on the

table. I use my fingers to pull the lips of her pussy apart. She's beautiful. All feminine heat that is slick, wet, pale pink with darker hues slowly fading in. *A work of art.* I blow across the tender flesh and watch the skin react, as her clit literally pulsates. I put two of my fingers against the needy little button. Then I slowly drag them over her clit and further down until I get to her entrance. There I push the fingers, which are now coated with her juices, into her tight channel. Again my dick reacts strongly by pushing up towards her like the desperate bastard he is. He wants inside her. *I want inside her.* I try to hold on to why I am denying myself. I've never had a problem with doing that before. I never lose sight of the prize and I keep a tight leash on my desires. Ana has already managed to get me to loosen the reins way too much. I will not take her pussy until things are clearer, ground rules are set, and her body is demanding me beyond anything she's experienced before. I want Ana bound to me … at least until I'm done with her.

I groan because her whole body physically shivers at my invasion. The walls of her pussy clamp down on my fingers, trying to pull them deeper inside. I begin moving them in and out of her, loving the way her juice pours from her and the wet sounds it makes as I fuck her slow and hard.

"More," she whimpers, her hands going up to palm her breasts. I watch, fascinated at the way her fingers bite into those plush mounds. The skin stretches as she pulls on her nipples. I should reprimand her for taking that privilege, but it's too beautiful to watch. It's so erotic I want to watch longer, but I can't resist her pull. I place a kiss against her clit and then slide my tongue around her sweet pussy, gathering all the cream I can find while I continue to fuck her with my fingers. When her body starts thrusting up to meet my fingers and her moans grow louder, I know she's near the edge.

"Are you close, pet?" I ask her, allowing my breath to fan over her pussy before sliding my tongue back against her clit and twirling it over and over, sucking it into my mouth.

"Yes," she whispers, her voice full of desperation as she tries to grab hold of her orgasm. "Oh God, Roman. I'm coming." The last part of her sentence is drawn out in a long whine of need.

I pull away, leaving my fingers inside of her, but refusing to move them.

"Did I give you permission to come, Ana?"

"What? No!" she cries, her body shaking so much I can watch how it quakes.

"You can't come until I tell you to, pet."

"Roman!"

"I'm going to play with you a little longer. If you're a good girl, I'll let you come."

"*Yes!*" she cries as I pull my fingers out and then thrust them back in. Her body bows, trying to latch on tight enough to give her what she needs. Every movement she makes is poetry. I thought she was beautiful dancing. It was nothing compared to this. *And her taste.* It's like nothing I've experienced before and far more addicting than any drug. I can't resist diving back in. I let my tongue move along the heated folds of her pussy, sliding my tongue inside with my fingers. I repeat that a couple of times, working in tandem to excite her even more, until I finally direct all of my attention back to her clit.

I know I'm pushing her past her limits. I know that she doesn't have the discipline needed to pass this test. I have no business even bringing her this far into my world without ground rules. I know all this, I just don't give a fuck. In my mind, I'm yelling, *Don't come, Ana,* even knowing she will. I have fallen under her spell. She's been so naturally submissive up to this point that I could forget this is new to her. I doubt she even realizes how truly submissive she is.

"Roman, I'm coming," she gasps, which is really her undoing, because now I push her further.

"Not yet, pet," I warn her before I suck her clit into my mouth, humming against the nub while pushing my fingers deep inside of her. I pull my fingers apart, stretching her just as my teeth bite into the tender flesh of her clit. The sting of pain throws her over the edge into a climax. I give her just a little more, allowing her to fully go over the edge. Then, it takes every bit of willpower I have to take my mouth and hand away, ensuring that her orgasm, though complete, never truly takes her where it could. It just leaves her needing more.

"Roman?" she asks, confused. Her violet eyes are smoky as she slowly opens them.

"I told you not to come," I tell her.

Shock fills her face. She shuffles to sit on the table. I use my hands on her hips to help brace her. "I... you... can't..."

"Now you have to be punished, Ana."

"Punished?" she squeaks.

"It's your first offense, so I'll go easy on you."

"Easy on me?" she parrots.

My thumb moves along her bottom lip, following the curve. I push against it, letting just the tip of my thumb push into her mouth.

"I'm going to fuck this pretty little face."

She doesn't respond, but I don't miss the way she squirms at my words.

She might be the most perfect partner I've ever played with.

17

I jerk awake with a start. I'm surprised I slept at all. I haven't been able to get more than a few hours a night since Allen started getting into trouble. Roman is sleeping beside me, his hand strung across my stomach. The temptation to stay is strong. The heat of his body lures me in, and there's so much more I want to experience. For all that we've done, I've not had him inside of me yet, and I ache for that. *Hunger for it.* I've had a few relationships and I've always known that I like for a man to take control, but none have been as dominate and demanding as Roman was. I even have the feeling that he was holding back. I would love to explore more with him. That would be bad. *For several reasons.*

I want to stretch against him and relax back into his warmth. I can't. I can't stay here. I need to meet with Paul and I need to see if he's managed to get any more leads on Allen. I can't help but stare at Roman for a minute. Asleep, he looks different. Still devastatingly handsome and breathtaking, but his face is softer, relaxed ... even peaceful. I've spent the last couple of days kicking myself for being attracted to Roman. It goes against everything I stand for. I know what kind of man he is. I know the things he does. All of that should make me run in the opposite direction. Yet, here I am in bed with him, breaking every rule I've put in place, and not even able to drum up enough guilt to care. In fact, if he was to wake up right now, I'd give myself to him again.

I should have never crossed that line. Now I'm afraid I'll never be able to go back.

I try to slide out of the bed, but Roman's hand stops me, pulling me back into him. At first I'm afraid I've woken him, but he mumbles and shifts in his sleep. I hold myself as still as humanly possible, but doing so causes me to breathe in his scent, and this tiny frisson of need blooms in my stomach and moves through my body. Good Lord, he's more addicting than any drug on the market. Once he settles down, I try once again to slide away. He protests at first, his fingers pressing into my side. No one has ever tried to hold on to me, in bed or out, and the fact that Roman is, really messes with my head.

I push it away. I can't fixate on that right now. I carefully replace my body with the pillow above my head and, inch by inch, pull away. It takes me awhile to gather my clothes, mostly because I keep looking back expecting Roman to catch me. *Insanity.* He'll probably be glad I'm going. He doesn't seem the type to indulge in awkward morning-after conversation.

I have my satchel, but I'm afraid to take the time to find clean clothes, so I put my underwear and bra back on in disgust. I've never done it before. Is this what makes the walk of shame so… *shameful?* Then, I hold the rest of the clothes and my overnight bag tight to my chest and carefully leave the room. I can get dressed with less worry in the living area. I'm pulling up my pants when I hear movement to my right. My eyes look up and that's when I see the maid from last night. She's shooting me a look much like I imagine Medusa would use when turning her victims to stone.

"Um… I was just going to…"

"Leave? Don't let me stop you. Mr. Anthes doesn't normally like his whores to be here when he wakes up, so you should hurry. The few that overstayed their welcome wish they hadn't."

I'm completely taken aback. Her words smack me harder than any physical blow would. If looks could kill, I would be dead.

"I'm sorry about the dishes. I could help." Even as I'm saying the words, I hate them, but I need to not make enemies. I do not need someone dying to destroy me, especially in Roman's home.

"The last thing I need is *your* help," she replies cattily.

Well, it can't get any clearer than that. I quickly put my shirt and socks on, then walk to the door.

"I'm sorry for the inconvenience," I say again. Really, at this point I want to kick my own ass.

"Just make sure you didn't steal anything. Mr. Anthes will not look kindly towards a thief."

Look kindly? Steal? *Thief?* There so much there to dislike and the words make me swallow the acid that has churned up from my stomach. I want to scream at her and maybe throat-punch her, kick her in the lady-junk. *Something.*

Instead, I ignore her, which is no consolation. I quietly open the door and step outside. I lean against it and take a large breath, feeling like I just escaped prison. My body jumps when I hear the click of the lock from the other side. The maid, no doubt. *Bitch.* I take a deep breath and then walk away. If I hurry, I'll have just enough time to shower before I meet Paul. The last thing I need is to go see him while smelling like sex—*like sex with Roman.* I can only imagine the lectures *that* will get me.

18
Ana

"The next time you decide to text me at six in the morning and ask me to meet you in thirty minutes, the least you could do is be on time, Ana," Paul says, his gravelly voice ringing out in the empty warehouse. We're meeting in an abandoned warehouse about three blocks from the apartment I'm renting. I think it used to be an old dog food factory. Now it's just empty cement that smells musty, dirty, and—just to add spice—seems to have a faint smell of urine. Whether it's human or animal, I couldn't begin to know, and don't care to find out.

"It's just ten minutes. Stop whining, Paul. You sound like an old mother hen," I tell him, grabbing the coffee he's handing me. *Coffee, sweet nectar of the gods.* It's the only thing that keeps me going these days.

"Someone needs to worry about shit around here. You sure aren't. What the hell do you think you're doing, Ana?"

I freeze with my lips against the plastic lid on the container and close my eyes. Shit. Fuck. Damn. *He knows.* "I don't know what you mean," I bluff. "I don't have much time though, so give me what you guys got at the raid yesterday."

"What are you doing, Ana?" he repeats, but his voice is softer this time, the type of voice I imagine a father using on his daughter. Well, a good one. I never had one of those, but I can imagine it. And Paul is everything I wish my father had been. At fifty-two, he's stern but caring, and has been a great role model. He's helped me turn my life around. So, it's not easy seeing the disappointment in his eyes right now.

"Please, Paul, let it go. Brass told me they wanted me to get close to Roman."

"They didn't mean his bed."

"That's not the first time a UC went beyond for a case. Don't try to convince me I'm wrong."

"It's not, but that doesn't make it right, and those guys have been with the DEA for fucking years; they're one step away from going vigilante. That's not who you want to model your career after. Shit, girl. You're a fucking beat cop. The higher-ups only put you in this position because it involved your brother."

"And it's working, right?"

"Ana."

"Paul, I have to try and get my brother out of this mess alive. If I can do that, that's all that matters."

"And kiss your career goodbye?"

"If that's what it takes."

"That's crazy talk, kid. You don't want to ruin your career over this. It doesn't matter what you do, your brother's still going to prison. You have to know that."

"Maybe that's the best thing for him. He can get clean behind bars," I argue. He gives me *that* look. The one that says I'm being naïve. Maybe I am. I know drugs are thick in the prisons too, but he stands a chance of getting clean there. If he stays free, he's going to die.

If he's not already dead.

"Ana, you need to face facts."

"Can you please just let this drop and tell me what they found in the raid?"

Paul sighs, but thankfully he lets it go. I know it's just a temporary reprieve, but still I'm grateful.

"Nothing, kid. Much like we thought. We only did it to distract him and try to rescue you without closing down the investigation. That obviously didn't work."

I concentrate on my coffee and ignore the heat in my face.

"You're having me tailed."

"You had to know that. You might be deep undercover, but there's no way they're going to trust you not to fuck shit up—and not just because you're Allen's sister."

"Because I'm a rookie."

"Because you're not even DEA. There's too much invested to rest it on an unknown."

"So there's someone else undercover besides me?"

Paul's silence speaks volumes. *Shit. Fuck. Damn.* I finish off the last of my coffee, going over the people I'm in contact with, trying to figure out who the fuck the other agent is. I sure as fuck don't need someone getting me pulled from this case. Shit, I don't want them to decide to close it down and bring Roman in either. Their first priority will *not* be my brother.

"We need you to take these and plant them in Roman's bedroom. It's the only room we've been unable to get a device in, undetected," Paul says, handing me a small white envelope.

"Same drill as before?" I ask, stuffing the paper into the front pocket of my jeans.

"Yeah, try to keep them as close to the bed as you can, or the desk in his room."

"Got it," I tell him, trying to ignore the way I feel guilt at doing my job. I didn't choose the life Roman has. I should have nothing to feel guilty about. *Nothing.*

"Try to remember that they're there, will you? The last fucking thing you need to do is have Brass hear you taking it up the ass by one of their most-wanted kingpins." I grow pale at his words. He's upset, I get that. I didn't expect *that* from him, however.

"I'll just be going, now," I tell him, turning away to leave.

He grabs my arm to stop me. "Ana, listen…"

I turn slightly so I can see him. "I think you've said enough. I appreciate the advice and concern, but at twenty-six, I will make my own decisions and live with the consequences. I don't need anyone talking down to me."

"Ana, you don't understand…"

"I'll check in tomorrow, Paul," I interrupt him and walk out with him saying my name to my back. I'm not mad, not really. He's right. I did let it go too far. He's also wrong because I didn't do it for Allen. I'm not about to tell him that, however. It's too late to go back and I don't want to. It's a moot point because as I jog around the corner heading towards my apartment, I see Roman standing on my doorstep, in his suit, coat, and gloves. He's angry, I can tell that even from this distance. What I notice most, however, is the way my pussy clenches and the butterflies in my stomach when he turns his gaze on me.

It's much too late to change anything.

19
Roman

I watch her jogging up to me like she doesn't have a care in the world. As beautiful as she is right now in her jeans and pale blue tank with her hair pulled up on top of her head, I want to spank her ass. She stops two steps down from where I'm perched by the door to her brownstone apartment.

"Where have you been, pet?"

"Running," she says, her voice breathless.

"Most people run in exercise clothes."

"Seemed like an expense I didn't need to worry about. I don't get to run that often." She shrugs.

It bothers me. Has she been going without to cover for her damned brother? She can't run in jeans. It will chaff the inside of her thighs, and since I now have plans for those beauties, that is unacceptable.

"You ran from my bed this morning."

"You were sleeping. It didn't seem right to wake you. I needed to get back to my apartment and start my day."

"You could have started it in my bed."

"I'm not sure that would have been a good idea."

"I'm positive it would have been," I tell her, sliding my fingers along the base of her neck and cupping the side of her face. "Because then I could have started my day *in* you." I watch as her eyes dilate as I bring her closer to my lips.

"I can see how that might have been … preferable," she whispers. Our lips are almost touching and her tongue darts out to lick against my bottom lip. I capture it, bringing it into my mouth. Somehow, her taste is even better this morning. I could be in trouble with this girl because just this has calmed the anger I had building inside me upon finding her gone. I deepen the kiss, letting my tongue play and becoming familiar with her again.

"That's better," I tell her when our lips break apart.

"Good morning to you, too," she tells me.

"You sneaking out on me is unacceptable, pet."

"I needed to get back to my world and find my brother," she says.

Her words put me on edge. "I told you I would help you do that."

"I know, but we kind of got distracted, and I know you just agreed to help me to—"

"To what?"

"Get in my pants."

"And you figure now that I've achieved that, I won't worry about your brother?"

"Something like that," she admits. I let my thumb move back and forth over her cheek, studying her. With any other woman, she'd be right.

"You gave yourself to me, pet. I'll take care of you, and that means helping you find your brother."

Her eyes study me and I can see distrust in her eyes. She has good reason to feel like that. It doesn't mean I like it, however.

"I'll trust you." *Why does it feel like she's telling much more than what her words are saying? What is this woman doing to me?* "Where do we start?" she asks.

"Breakfast, pet. Then we'll discuss business."

For a second I think I see disappointment in her eyes, but she nods her agreement. I take a step away from her, which isn't easy. I hold out my hand, and something shifts inside of me when she places her small hand in mine and squeezes it.

76

20
Roman

"Roman, people are staring," Ana complains.

We're sitting in the middle of a breakfast chain restaurant. A type of place I can't say I've stepped foot in for years. I let Ana pick where we went and from the look in her eyes, I know she thought she would shake me with her choice. What she doesn't realize is that things like this might be one of the reasons she appeals to me so deeply. According to the menu, our entire meal will probably be covered with twenty bucks. The women before her would have picked a place where twenty dollars wouldn't have covered the tip.

"You're imagining it, pet."

"Not hardly, Anthes. Is there a reason you always insist I sit in your lap?"

"Anthes?"

She smirks, putting a forkful of pancakes in my mouth. The blueberry and sugary syrup combine in my mouth, and though it's good, it's not even a comparison to the taste of Ana. "If it bothers you, imagine I'm calling you Daddy. Or do you prefer Master?"

The little minx. She's full of sass and I apparently love it because my dick is demanding its turn at training her. My lips find her ear and she giggles, pulling her head down to try and halfheartedly get away. My fingers dig into her thigh at the same time that my teeth bite into her earlobe. She gasps from the small dose of pain, and I feel a gentle shudder travel through her body.

"Roman," she murmurs, and motherfucker, if my dick isn't leaking on my leg.

"You're tempting me to show you who is in charge, right here in the middle of this restaurant. Keep it up, pet, because I would like nothing better than to fuck you."

"You wouldn't," she answers, but I can hear the doubt in her words as her entire body goes still.

"In a fucking heartbeat," I assure her and I'm completely serious.

"Maybe we should talk about something else," she suggests, and the look on her face is so sweet that I kiss her on the lips. Her tongue pushes into my mouth, deepening the kiss, and I let her explore while I take another hit of her addictive flavor. I was right; she's definitely more potent than any drug.

When I break the kiss, I pick up one of the sausage links, forgetting my fork. I bring it to her lips and she opens, deliberately taking the food inside and wrapping her tongue around it as she goes. Her ass wiggles around on my lap, torturing my cock. She plays for a few more minutes, purposefully teasing with the food, before eating it.

"You keep wiggling around like that and we're going to have a repeat of what happened during your dance. While I did love it, the next time I come it will be inside of you."

Her cheeks somehow blush again. I'm getting used to this, how her almost innocent side mixes with the wicked woman and constantly entertains me. I'm starting to think she might be the first woman I've ever met who will never bore me. A woman like that is someone you could ... *keep*. That's insane though. I'm not that man. It's time I bring this conversation around to something which will keep her from working her spell on me. She's different, but she's just a woman.

"Tell me how you found out your brother was missing."

She stiffens in my arms, and I hate that I took the playful look off her face. I'm even starting to hate the fact that I'm the fucker who has her brother.

"Allen always disappears. I've grown used to it. He fell into the wrong crowd when we were younger and despite everything I tried, I wasn't able to pull him back. I've been losing my brother for years."

"And you still are trying to find him?"

"He's my brother. The only family I have."

"What if he gets you hurt in the meantime?"

"I can take care of myself. Been doing it for a long time now."

I don't like that reply. I don't like it at all. There's fuck-all I can say, though.

"Where was the last place he was seen?" I ask, even as I'm kicking myself. What would she do if I took her to her brother now? He's slowly healing. I didn't want him looking as if he was a step away from death, in case I had to show him to Ana. I'm not desperate enough to use him to get Ana in my bed; I knew I could manage that on my own. But to keep her from getting the police into checking my club out and other things in hopes of finding him? That's the reason—and the *only* reason—her brother is still drawing air.

"Your club, The Stable." It takes all my years of playing poker and bluffing my way out of tight spots combined not to react. "It's why I started working for you in the first place. The Stable wasn't hiring. I had dancing experience. Dive was hiring."

"How did you know I owned both?"

She shrugs, taking a drink of her coffee. "That was a coincidence. I had been living in Boca, a little over an hour from here. I needed a job here in Miami that would pay decent and keep me in the general area. It worked out."

"Conveniently," I answer, making a note to have my man track down more info about her being in Boca. I didn't recall that in the file Joe showed me.

"I'm not going to lie, Roman. I'm glad it did, and not just because of my brother," she whispers.

"Really?" I ask, letting myself get lost in the look in her eyes. My hand slides along the inside of her thigh, stopping just an inch from her pussy. The heat I feel from her even through her jeans is intense. The muscles in her thighs tighten under my hand.

"Really," she whispers.

"I'll get my people working on trying to track your brother down." Her body goes tense in my arms.

"You mean it?"

"I don't waste my time saying things I don't mean, pet. You need to prepare yourself, though; if he's as far gone as you say he is, there might not be any saving him." Her violet eyes go sad and I find myself wishing I was a different person, a man who could slay dragons for her. Fuck. I need inside her so these damn reactions to her will stop. The best remedy I've found for almost anything is to fuck it out of your system. Ana is just one more in a list. Fucking her until I grow bored will be more pleasurable than anything I've done before.

"Roman?" she asks, that pretty little tongue of hers coming out to catch a drop of syrup on her lip.

"Yes, pet?"

"Take me home."

Her voice is husky, and those damn eyes of hers are liquid. I know what she needs, but I want the words.

"Why, Ana?"

"I need you to fuck me," she says bluntly, and though her voice is soft, the people around us can hear and she doesn't seem to give a damn. I throw a hundred on the table and stand up, bringing Ana with me. Her body is close to mine, her legs wrapped around my hips, her hands hugging my neck while she buries her head in my chest. The sound of the chair I was sitting in, scraping and rocking from my quick movements are echoed, because the room goes silent. I walk her straight out to the limo, ignoring everyone but Ana.

21
Ana

Roman somehow manages to fit his wide frame and mine through the door of the limo. He even manages to get the car door closed. That's good because I immediately go to my knees on the floor, undoing his tie and unbuttoning his shirt. I get the top part of his chest exposed, then stretch up to drag my tongue along the skin, licking and placing gentle kisses. I'm hoping if I distract him enough that he forgets about the fucking slip I made.

It was a damned rookie mistake. How could I have said he was the reason I started working at Dive? I hope I covered good enough, but the minute the words left my mouth, I saw questions in Roman's face. So I did what women everywhere have been doing for years: I distracted him with sex.

It's just one more thing for Paul to throw in my face later.

I can't worry about that right now, because what started out as distraction has turned into a wildfire that is definitely out of control. I start to work on more buttons, eager to taste the salty male flavor that is Roman. He stops me by wrapping his fist in my hair and yanking my head back hard. My heart rockets into my throat thinking I've failed and he's about to interrogate me about our conversation. I'm so fucked up over Roman. I'd never admit it to Paul, but I'm losing sight of the reason I'm here. I'm losing sight that this is about my own brother, so much so that when he pulls my hair so violently that the rough pain shoots through my body, my pussy quakes with need. I can feel the effect he has on me by the way the insides of my thighs grow wet.

"Undo my pants," his dark voice orders.

His eyes are deep and intense and they spear through me. I swallow nervously as I bring my hands to his belt, unlatching. My eyes drift back up to his as I slip the top button of his slacks loose and then carefully slide the zipper down. The look on his face is beautiful. It's almost as if he's in pain. I want to keep looking but his cock instantly springs out, demanding attention. There's so much to be said about a man going commando, and all of it is good.

I bend down to run my tongue up the front of his cock when he pulls hard on my hair again. "Did I say you could have my cock, pet?"

The tone of his voice, the look on his face, and the way he keeps demanding I ask for permission all combine together and explode inside of me in a way that sends shockwaves through my body that all detonate in my pussy and causes a mini-orgasm. I shiver in response. "No, Roman," I tell him, my voice in a tone I have never heard from myself before. It's so full of need.

"You must learn who is in control. Lock your hands behind your back, grab your wrists, and no matter what, you keep them there. Understand?"

Just like that, my breath goes ragged. I put my hands behind my back and do as he instructed. He gets a ghost of a smile on his face. I want to keep watching it, but my eyes are pulled back to his cock as he holds it in his hand. Everything about Roman is larger than life, but when his hand wraps around the base of his cock, it does nothing but accentuate how truly large he is. He pulls me in close, close enough that his dick is right there but I have to reach to touch it. I do it automatically, but at the first sting of pain, I look up at him instinctively. He nods his head in agreement to a question I wasn't even aware I was asking. I strain against his hold to run my tongue up the front of his shaft. It pulls my hair; he's not giving me an inch of movement, but his groan encourages me to keep pushing. When I reach the head of his dick and the taste of his pre-cum gathers on the tip of my tongue, I moan. I fight harder against his restraint to take just the tip into my mouth. I close my lips against him, sucking hard while my tongue tries to find that small valley where more of his pre-cum is. I want more. I *need* it like I need my next breath. When he doesn't let my mouth slide further, I pull away.

"Roman," I whimper, sounding desperate. How did I get here this quickly? How can I need him so deeply? It's as if he has become a missing element in my life that I need to breathe. Food. Sleep. Air. *Roman*. He's becoming that essential. I block out the warning bells that admission sets off.

"Patience, pet," his voice grumbles.

I want to yell, but I don't. He brings his cock to my mouth and pushes his shaft against it. His hand tightens in my hair, preventing me from taking him inside. Instead, he moves it along my lips, painting them with the evidence of his need. Just when I'm about to scream, he pushes his cock inside my mouth. I hum my approval around it. I have very little control, but he allows me to sink lower on his shaft. He's so wide that it's almost painful to close my lips around him. I let my tongue play with him and suck him until he's halfway in my mouth. That's as much as I can comfortably take. Then, I glide back up. I repeat over and over, hearing Roman whispering soft praises in the background. With each note of approval, I take him a little more until his dick is at the back of my throat.

I gag around him and Roman is quick to back out. He stops me when his tip is still at my lips. "You have to learn to take all of me, Ana. I'm not going to want to go without your mouth."

Wrong or not, his words make another quake of excitement rumble through me. Determined to show him I can take whatever he gives me, when he pushes my head back down on his shaft, I do my best to position my tongue so that when I take him to the back of my throat, my gag reflex doesn't get triggered. I hum around his cock when I feel him leaking down my throat. I breathe through my nose, my eyes going to his. The look in his eyes spurs me on and I swallow, letting the motion of my throat muscles convulse against his head. His fingers flex in my hair and he groans. It probably sounds silly, but that simple noise he gives me makes me feel like I am the most beautiful woman in the world.

Now he takes over, pulling my head back and pushing it down in a steady rhythm. He starts slow and I have time to use my tongue to tease him. My mission is to push him over the edge, to make him lose that tight leash he keeps on himself. His speed increases then, almost violently, and I can do nothing but take it as he rams his cock in and out of my mouth. He's in control of everything. *He's in control of me.* I try to watch the changes in him because I know he's getting close, but it's impossible. I'm consumed with the way he fills my mouth, the hard veins that are throbbing and pulsating, his taste filling me. He uses his cock as a weapon, fucking my face hard. My body is a bundle of nerves and the slightest touch would set me off and he's not even touched me.

"I'm getting ready to come, Ana. I'm going to come and fill that pretty mouth and you're going to suck it all down. Swallow every fucking drop. Do you hear me, pet?" he growls, holding my head still.

I'd talk if I could, but my mouth is full of dick—*of Roman*. In the end, all I can do his hum my agreement. That seems to be enough because he thrusts me down on his shaft again and again before erupting with a growl. His cum slides down my throat in waves and I open my eyes to watch as the climax moves through him. *Beautiful.*

22
Roman

I pull Ana up beside me. She stretches out on the seat, rubbing against me like a cat begging to be petted. Her head rests in my lap against my undone pants. Her hair is ruffled and finally completely out of order. It's much hotter than I even imagined. I run my fingers through it while I catch my breath. I hit the intercom when I finally remember I have yet to tell Robert where to take us.

"Robert, takes back to Ana's apartment."

"Yes, sir," he responds and I click it off.

"My apartment?"

"It's closer and I need you in a bed, pet," I tell her, not bothering to expand. The plain truth is that if I don't get inside of her soon, my dick is going to drive me mad. I just came inside of that sweet mouth of hers and I'm still hard as a hammer. There's only so much control a man can have—even me.

She pulls my shirt up and places a kiss against my stomach before sitting up. Regretfully, I fix my pants, adjusting my damn dick because we should be at her apartment in about fifteen minutes.

"We'll have to hurry. I'll need to get to work so I have time to run through my sets and pick out the costumes and things."

"I don't think so."

"Roman," she starts, and my hand goes to the side of her neck and I pull her face into mine, my grip not hard enough to hurt her, but firm enough so that she is reminded who's in charge.

"My woman doesn't strip for other men, Ana."

"Your woman? Listen Roman, we just started seeing each

other and you knew I was a stripper before this started!"

"We're doing a hell of a lot more than just seeing each other. My cock was just in that throat of yours. My cum is in your stomach. If you think I'm going to let you dance for another man after the dance you gave me in that room, Ana, you're fucking crazy."

Her head snaps back, but I just increase my hold on her, not letting her pull away.

"That was different! I don't dance for other men! I told you that! Of all the pigheaded, egotistical, juvenile—"

"Ana, that's *enough.* I didn't mean that you would. I'm just telling you that I've claimed this body and there's not another man out there who's going to get a look at what is mine. And, pet, let us be clear: *you are mine.*"

She goes still, but most of all she shuts up. "You don't know me."

"I know all I need to know and I plan on learning much more."

"You might not like what you find."

"And I may like it even more," I tell her.

She's cute. Is she worried that her past is something that will bother me? That I will hold it against her? It's her that needs to learn who I am. I'll teach her that, too. *In time.* It's occurred to me that what I'm talking about is something more than just sex. I'm not going to spend time thinking about it. I want her and it's not showing signs of lessening. Actually, something that has never happened to me in my lifetime is going on. The more I'm around Ana, the more I want her. I'm not growing bored. I'm showing no signs of boredom. Usually one time is enough to take off the new, wear the edge down. Maybe it's because I haven't actually been inside of her yet. Fuck if I know; I just know nothing is happening like I thought it would. I have a sneaking suspicion Ana is a game-changer.

"What am I supposed to do if I don't work? Jesus, Roman, I *have* to work. I have bills and I like having a roof over my head. Besides that, I'm not one to sit around and do nothing. I've worked since I was sixteen."

"You'll live with me."

"I can't—Wait a minute. What did you say?"

"You don't need to worry about a roof over your head. You'll stay under my roof."

"I can't move in with you! We just met."

"I've had my face buried between your legs and my dick in your mouth. I think that means more than how long we've actually known each other."

"*That's* what you're basing asking a woman to move in with you on? Because we got each other off? Jesus, your house must be crowded. Where do you keep all of the women?"

"You're entirely too mouthy for my peace of mind, pet. Believe it or not, there's never been another woman in my house. For you, I'm making an exception. I have a feeling it won't be the first."

"Mouthy? I'd take exception to that, but I think you just shocked me into silence."

"I'm not sure that's possible."

Ana does something else that shocks me. She sticks her tongue out at me. For the first time that I can remember in what has to be years, I throw my head back and laugh.

"You're really beautiful when you laugh, Roman," Ana whispers softly.

I bring my eyes back to her face at her words and take in the sweet way she's looking at me. Men would go off to war and die, all for the chance to protect that face. I pull her to me and take her mouth. Five minutes. *Five minutes* until we get to her apartment and then I'm fucking her brains out.

My cell phone rings in my pocket and I pull away from Ana after dragging my tongue against hers one last time. I look at my phone. When I see Bruno's number, I know I'm in trouble.

"Yeah?" I grunt, answering it.

"Boss, we got problems."

"I'm getting fucking tired of hearing that."

"The warehouse was just broken into."

"What happened to the guards?" I growl, anger rolling through me.

"Two dead. Four unconscious."

My hand tightens up on the phone. I'd like to throw the damn thing. "Who are the two who died?"

"Ivan and Reese."

"Fuck," I groan, holding my head down. "Have you told their families?"

"No, boss. I just called the rest of the cleanup crew out and called you."

"Any idea who did it?"

"They were gone when we got here, but, boss…"

"Spit it out, Bruno, what did the cameras show?"

"One of the security cameras, the new one we put in across the street, showed Banks."

"I'll be there in five. I want the cleaning crew called out and I'll go talk to Ivan's wife. Reese didn't have anyone but his mother. She's still in that nursing home. I'll go there tomorrow. Keep a lock on this shit. The last thing these ladies need to hear is about their men before I can talk to them."

"You got it," Bruno says and I hang up.

I turn to look at Ana and worry is etched all over her face.

"I take it our plans have changed," she says as the car comes to a stop.

"I'm sorry, Ana. I can't."

"It's okay, Roman. Go do what you have to do. I'll be here when you get back," she tells me as Robert opens the door.

I cup her face in my hand. "I'll be back as soon as I can."

Her hand moves over my wrist that is resting on her collarbone. She squeezes it, encouragingly. "Someone died?" she questions, and I fight against my need to reassure her. I can't trust anyone—especially a woman—with my business, no matter how the look in her eyes makes me want to trust her.

"Two of my men," I answer, compromising. Even giving her that much makes me want to kick my ass.

Ana doesn't push me, however. She leans up and kisses me lightly on the cheek, and then stretches up to whisper in my ear. "Be safe, *Daddy*."

The whispered words make me want to smile. I would if I didn't know what was waiting for me. I watch as she slides out of the car. It's not until I'm ten minutes down the road that I realize I didn't walk her to her door and make sure she was safe. I've never felt the urge to before, but I vow that will never happen again. *Ana's mine.* I'm keeping her.

23
Ana

I lean against the door when I make it inside. My emotions are all over the place. Being near Roman makes me forget what I'm really here for. That's dangerous. It's also extremely stupid. Roman's a job. I'm here to find evidence on him and save my brother. It's that simple. The rest is just static. I can't allow it to get to me. I can't allow Roman to get to me. After giving myself a pep talk, I start walking up the stairs to my apartment when a hand reaches out and grabs me from behind. I scream before I can stop myself and years of training takes over. I step into my attacker, deliver an elbow back into his solar plexus. I hear a male grunt and I reach behind my head and wrap my arms around my attacker's neck, flipping him over my shoulder. He lands with a thud, groaning and still holding his stomach.

"Told you not to sneak up on her, rookie," I hear Paul say from my left.

The adrenaline is still surging through me, but that's when I can recognize the guy on the floor as one of the main officers who work underneath Paul.

"What the hell are you two doing here? Are you trying to blow my cover?"

"Gee, Ana, it's not like we planned on you bringing that slime back home with you. I told you, kid, you're skating on thin ice here."

"Back off, Paul. I'm doing what I have to do to make sure my brother survives this shit."

"Whatever helps you sleep at night," the man on the floor wheezes as he gets up. I instantly want to knock him back down.

"What do you want? You do realize Roman could be having me watched?"

"You're safe. We've cleared all the security."

"Whatever. Tell me what you did. Before we got here, Roman got a call that something had happened. He mention deaths. Why did he mention deaths, Paul?"

"We raided the warehouse. There were more guards there than we anticipated. They surprised a few of our men. It had to be done."

"No, it didn't. Why are you doing that? I thought the reason I'm undercover is so we can know what property to check into and not do stupid shit and get people killed. *People like my brother!*"

"I thought that was the reason you were here too, Ana. But it seems to me the reason is all about you fucking the enemy now."

"You need to step back, Paul. I'm doing what I have to do to take care of my brother and do my job. You may not like it, but you better damn well respect me and keep your judgments to yourself," I growl, having enough of the shit he keeps dishing out. It may be frowned on, but if I was a male officer, it wouldn't even be a question. He'd be patting me on the back. "I am doing my job, and if you would just let me work and give me time, then maybe we wouldn't have to kill innocent people!"

"They're not innocent, Ana. They're felons. Scum of the earth that are supplying drugs to—"

"They are human beings and one of them had a wife and a mother. Last I checked, our job was to protect and serve, not kill and leave lying and shrug it off."

"If you're done being on your high horse, I don't have much time here."

My stomach churns with the look on Paul's face. Why had I never noticed this side of him before? Something about his whole attitude makes me feel like my skin is crawling. Something is just… *off.*

"Say it," I tell him, just wanting him to leave. He hands me a small packet of white powder. I look at it like it's a snake, one that's about to bite me and pump my body full of poison. "What the fuck is this?"

"Coke."

I blanch, physically jarred from his answer, even if I knew what it was. "Why are you giving this to me?" I whisper, that sick feeling in the pit of my stomach only getting worse.

"You need to plant that on Anthes."

"Plant? What are you talking about?"

"The fucking weasel keeps covering his tracks and he slips through every fucking trap we set. We get him on possession, he'll get out, but it will give us all the ammo we need to get a judge to give the okay to take a fine-tooth comb to his businesses and anything else. It will give us time to sweep in and tear apart his business piece by piece."

"Paul, that's … what you're asking me to do …"

"Before you go all moral, that's just enough to cap him for possession. It's enough to get our fucking foot in the door. It will save your brother. The quicker we get Anthes locked up, the quicker we can find your brother."

"But…" I try and argue, but my tongue feeling too heavy for my mouth and refuses to form words. My heart is beating erratically and I am about two steps away from a panic attack.

"Your brother is running out of time, Ana. Do you really want to be the reason for his death?" he asks, then motions to the guy with him. They leave me standing there looking like I was just in a train wreck and holding an eight ball of coke and wondering how the fuck I got here.

24

Ana

I jerk awake in bed and reaching for the pistol I keep under my pillow. I grab the butt of the grip, wrapping my fingers around it, when a large hand clamps down making it so I can't move.

"Jesus Christ, Ana. You keep a gun under your fucking pillow?"

I go deathly still in the dark of my bedroom. "Roman?"

"Who the fuck else would it be getting into your bed at three in the morning?" he asks, taking the gun away from me and placing it on my nightstand.

That's a good question. "Roman? How are you in my bed? You don't have a key. You gave me a heart attack!"

"I could tell by the way you were about to shoot me. Motherfucker, what the hell has happened to you in the past that you sleep with a gun under your pillow?"

That's a question I'm not about to answer. "Will you tell me how you got in?" I ask instead, my eyes following his body and enjoying the view. Roman is probably the sexiest man I've ever met in my life. Roman without a shirt is deadly. He might be covered up too, but shivers run through me when I realize he's probably completely naked and in my bed.

"Pet, you'll find there's not much I can't do when I want it. And I think we've established that I want you. Now let's get back to the question at hand. Why do you sleep with a gun under your pillow?" he asks, and I try to ignore the distraction of a naked Roman to concentrate on our conversation.

"I'm a single woman alone in the city," I compromise. It

sounds plausible? *Right?*

"If I get my hands on your brother, I may choke the life out of him for leaving you in the position where you think you need a gun to protect yourself."

I listen to him and there's a lot to think about in that one sentence. Most of all, it sounds like he hasn't killed my brother. Maybe it's not him that has Allen at all. *Could the informant have been wrong?* On the heels of that thought is the warm feeling I get inside at the fact that Roman is concerned about me. No one ever has been, except Paul ... and now I wonder if he ever really was. If we had the relationship I thought we had, would he have put me in the situation I am in right now? The Paul I had created in my mind would have never done anything underhanded.

I push thoughts of Paul out of my head. I can't deal with that right now. I have the coke locked in a firebox under my bed. Fuck if I know what I'm going to do. As I look at Roman now and see how tired and upset he looks, pain squeezes my heart.

"You had a bad night," I tell him. It's not a question; the truth of it is written all over his face.

"Yeah, pet. It was a bad night."

"Do you want to talk about it?"

"There's a reason I don't do relationships, Ana. You get what I do, everything I am. It's not a normal nine-to-five, nor is it what most people could accept. I have my own laws, my own code..."

"Roman, everyone has the same laws."

"No, pet. They don't. But it doesn't concern you."

"If we're dating..."

"I told you, I don't—"

"Whatever we're doing, we seem to be heading in a direction where—"

"Where we're going to fuck over and over?"

I smile, despite the gravity of the situation facing me. I feel like a fraud, even as a larger part of me wants to believe that I'm having this conversation because somehow I'll get to keep Roman. *I think I really want to keep him.*

"Freak. I was going to say it looks like we may be spending more time together."

"Oh yeah, definitely spending more time together."

I shake my head at him. "Roman, I'm serious. If we keep seeing each other, your life and choices will affect me. Don't you think I need to know more? To prepare myself, if nothing else?"

"We're definitely going to keep seeing each other, Ana," he says, cupping the side of my face. He seems to do that a lot, and I'm not going to lie. Every time he does, a small piece of the distance I try to keep between us chips away. "And nothing I do will ever touch you, pet. I'm starting to realize you aren't used to having a real man in your life, but you're mine," he says and the words vibrate through in a way that causes every single female part inside of me to clench in pleasure. *Can you orgasm without any kind of sex?* "I've claimed you and I will protect you from everything, including myself. Nothing will touch you."

Wow. If only he could, but he can't. He has no idea who I am, and he thinks I don't know anything about him. Our relationship, or whatever this is, has all been built on a house of cards and I'm the dealer. What will Roman do when he finds out he's being played?

I bring my hand up to cover his and pull it to my lips to kiss his palm. "It's too late to be having this type of conversation and you look worn out. Let's get some rest and worry about tomorrow, tomorrow," I urge him. I really can't handle any more heart-to-heart tonight.

"Ana, I've been wanting you under me all night. If you think I'm going to be satisfied with just sleep, you're dreaming."

"Noted. But first, we need to make you less tense."

"Sex does that."

"So does a backrub."

"A backrub?"

"You sound doubtful, but these hands," I tell him, holding my hands up and cracking my knuckles. *"These hands* are miracle workers."

"Is that a fact?"

"Completely. Now lay down on your stomach," I order him, getting up from the bed to grab a bottle of lotion. I make note to go shopping tomorrow to get some massage oil, preferably heated. It wasn't something I foresaw me needing before now. I go to the dresser, finding the lotion. I stop before I make it back to the bed. Roman is lying on his stomach, his head turned to watch me. He has the strangest look on his face. "What?" I ask, wondering if I've given myself away. Could I have pushed too much? *Does he suspect something?*

"Pet, are those ... unicorns with rainbows coming out of their ass ... on your pajamas?"

"Um ... maybe?"

He keeps staring at me, and I'm blushing like crazy. I don't need to see my face to know I am.

"Have I mentioned how you might be the first woman to surprise me? And you seem to do it constantly." He means that as compliment, I know he does, but the guilt that swamps me makes it impossible to respond. Instead, I clear my throat and try to offer a weak smile. I place some lotion on my hands and rub them together to warm up the cold cream, then I start working it into his lower back. Carefully, I make my way up his back, applying pressure on the tense muscles beneath. "That feels so good, pet. You might be magic."

"Told you," I whisper, my heart feeling heavy as I'm

swamped with so many different emotions that I'm having trouble functioning. We continue like that for a few more minutes until I finally gather up the courage to ask Roman a question that I really need the answer to. "Roman? What happened to the men you were talking about earlier? How did they die?"

Silence answers me. Did I push him to open up too soon?

"Roman?" I ask again, and there's a soft snore following my words. I look down and Roman is definitely sleeping. Guess my hands worked too well.

Disappointment swamps me. I didn't have a lot of expectations, but I was hoping to learn more about Roman because I need to trust and believe in him. The truth is, no matter how much I try to explain it away, Roman matters.

He matters a lot.

25

Roman

Apparently life with Ana is going to be a constant surprise. Never have I passed out on a woman. Yet with Ana, I did easily. I reach over for her, determined to have her finally. My hand finds nothing but her pillow and it's cold. I sit up, stretching, and let my eyes get adjusted to the darkness in the room. There's minimal light coming through the window. The clock tells me it's a little after six in the morning. The apartment is quiet; no obvious sounds telling me where she's at.

"Ana, where the hell are you?" I growl, grabbing my pants and putting them on before looking through the apartment for her. Each room comes up empty until it's apparent she's nowhere to be found. I'm about to tear from her place to search for her when I look through the glass doors that lead out to her balcony. Ana is sitting in a lounge chair wrapped up in a blanket and looking out over the sunrise. "I'm going to start tying you to the bed so I stop waking up alone. What are you doing out here?"

She looks up at me in surprise. I notice the tears in her eyes and they bother me. Am I the reason for them? Most likely. I'm really going to have to do something about this brother of hers if I keep her. *If.* I'm not letting her go. There's no point in hiding from that fact. I want her more than I did the first time and I've yet to get inside her. I can only imagine that once I get a taste of that, I'm doomed. *Brought down by a pussy.*

"Thinking."

I pick her up and slide underneath her on the lounge chair. The blanket drops to the floor, but I let it go. I figure I can keep her warm enough. I hold her head close to my chest and let my fingers brush through her hair. "You okay, pet?" I ask, knowing better.

"I'm a mess, Roman."

"Do you want to talk about it?"

"Not even a little bit."

We sit there in the silence a few more minutes while the sun breaks free from the clouds and its light blooms in the sky. She turns from her side, laying with her stomach pressed to mine, her face mere inches from me. I run my thumb over her chin, sweeping it up towards her cheek.

"You're beautiful, Ana."

"You weren't what I expected," she whispers in return. I'm not quite positive how to take that, so in the end I say nothing. Her fingers reach for the zipper of my slacks. I had left the top button undone, and in just a second she has them all undone. My cock, which had been semi-sleeping since finding Ana gone, begins to stretch and push towards her. I grab her hand to stop her.

"Ana."

"Please, Roman. Later, you can remind me you're in control. For now, just right now, can I take what I want? What I need?"

There's something in her eyes as she asks that question. Something that I vow to question further. When she pulls my shirt off and throws it on the ground, I stop thinking about it. As the sun's glow serves as a backdrop, highlighting her perfect body, I almost forget to breathe. When she pulls on my pants, I lift up and she works them past my hips. As she adjusts her legs to ride me and starts sliding back and forth on my cock, using the hard ridge of it to push against her pussy, I stop thinking altogether. I can feel the slick, wet heat of her desire paint my cock as she slowly drags herself back and forth.

"Fuck, pet. You're soaked."

"I need you," she gasps, moving her body back and using her hand to grasp the base of my cock.

"Then take me. For now, take what you want," I tell her, repeating her words and giving her the permission she needs.

26
Ana

Guilt can suffocate you. Roman has been so sweet, so loving, and he's nothing like the man I expected to encounter. He's good. He's a good man. I know he's involved in things that are bad, but the Roman I'm beginning to know is … *good*. What do I do with that? It's like I've fallen out of reality here. The rules have all changed and the bad guy isn't really the bad guy and the good guy clearly isn't good. And me … I'm stuck in the middle.

I need to save my brother. I have a job to do. But I never thought my job would mean I had to hurt innocent people. My brain wants to argue that Roman is far from innocent, but he would be innocent of what Paul asked me to set him up for. Paul—my mentor, the man I looked up to among all others, and he's asked me to go against everything I believe, every oath I ever made and everything I thought I was in the force to prevent. Paul's right. Roman's not innocent. But if we do this—if *I* do this—aren't we worse?

My head is a mess, and when Roman came out to find me and was so sweet, I was so close to jumping off the ledge, telling him everything that's going on and asking him to not only save my brother, but to save me. I can't take the final step to do that. What if I'm just losing sight of reality, lost in all that's Roman? If that's the case, I'm probably doing the last thing I should. *Losing myself even more.*

I brace my hands on his shoulders, riding back and forth on his cock, coating him in … *me.* His hard shaft slides between the lips of my pussy so easily, and it pushes up against my clit in all the right ways. I could come just like this, but I allow myself one truth in whatever this is I'm doing with Roman. *I need him inside of me.* I move back at his permission and wrap my hand around the base of his cock. My knees dig into the cushion of the chair as I rise above him. My eyes find his as I position him at my opening. His cock is so hot, so large. I know doing this might be wrong. Maybe that's what makes it even better. Maybe nothing matters except this moment. I lower myself slowly onto his shaft. I stop when just his head is inside of me. Just that much, and I already feel how he's going to stretch me beyond anything I've ever experienced. He may ruin me for other men. *He might have, already ...*

"Fuck, Ana," Roman groans, his hips thrusting up towards me as he sinks another inch inside. I gasp at the sensation as he sinks into me a little more. My fingers dig into his shoulders and the pleasure mixes with the sting of pain it takes to stretch around him and take him all the way inside. Once he's seated deep, I hold still and just get used to the feeling of being stretched and full of nothing but Roman. His hand slides under my hair and he holds the side of my face again, his thumb brushing against my skin as he does so often. "You okay, pet?"

Okay? No, I answer in my mind. Right now, I want my first time with Roman to be about nothing but him and me, so I push everything else away. I squeeze my inner muscles around his cock instead, bringing the focus back to the here and now, to the only thing that Roman and I can share.

"I feel so much better than okay," I moan as I lift back off his cock, slowly dragging him out of me, but keeping the tip, and then pushing back down. Roman's hands bite into my ass cheeks. They're not gentle, but even that feels good. No. It feels better than good. He's letting me be in charge, but not letting me forget that he is the one *really* in control. This time when I rise and lower myself back down, I do it at an angle and moan as his hard cock scrapes against my walls. Over and over I ride him, losing sight of everything but Roman's face, and the pleasure, and the look in his eyes. Everything else fades away. Faster and faster I get, lifting off and then taking him back in, pummeling my pussy with his dick—*using him*. I can feel my orgasm and it's right there. I can feel it. I can almost taste it, but can't quite reach it.

That's when Roman takes over. "You're so fucking beautiful, pet," his hoarse voice tells me, and even that feels like a caress. He uses his hold on my hips to take over the speed and angle of my ride. I turn over control willingly. My hands move to my breasts, clutching underneath them and holding onto them tightly. He slams me back down on his cock *hard*, so hard it physically jars my body and heat swamps me. I squeeze him inside of me as tight as I can. My head goes back from the pleasure.

"Roman," I cry out, feeling his dick so far in me that it's pressing against my cervix. It's painful but it also releases these shockwaves and ripples of pleasure inside of me that I've never known. I bend my body backwards, trying to stretch it to hold onto every sensation. Roman must know what I'm doing, or maybe he feels it too, because his bruising hold on me keeps me pushed down on him and then he grinds me against him. "Oh fuck!" I scream when he does it again.

"So beautiful, Ana," he repeats. "Come for me. Come for me, pet," Roman's voice growls, but I've lost sight of him. I'm riding wave after wave of pleasure and my orgasm shoots through me. Roman pulls me back off his dick and then slams me back down. I straighten and concentrate on the pleasure and the ride, my eyes closed. Shock courses through me as his lips latch onto one of my breasts and he bites into the nipple. My fingers dig into his hair as his mouth works its magic. His fingers slide into my ass and press against the opening. He holds me still this time, but thrusts his hips up into me. I grind down and meet his thrust, turning just enough so he's once again scraping my inner walls. That triggers a second orgasm which is so much more massive than the first. It sends wave after wave of pleasure through my body. I let out a long keening cry like I've never uttered before. I'm almost unsure it's me. When I feel the heat of his cum flood inside of me, it does nothing but add to the pleasure. My eyes fasten onto him. His dark eyes grow intense, glowing and full of pleasure as he gives in to his climax. His hand wraps in my hair and he pulls my head down to him.

"Mine," he growls. "You're mine, Ana."

His words feel like a brand, as hot and as heated as the cum he's shooting inside of me. The tears come without warning. They fall unchecked as he takes my mouth.

I could love him ...

27
Roman

"Damn it, Bruno, you better start getting it together or I'll find someone else who can."

"Got it, boss," he says before shaking his head and leaving the room. I'm taking out my frustration on him. It's not right, but that's definitely what I'm doing. I'm so fucking keyed up over Ana, I don't know which end is up. I've thought of little else since I left her this morning. That's how fucking twisted in knots she has me. It's ridiculous. It's also why I'm looking at her lowlife piece of shit brother instead of working like I need to be doing.

"Why are you still letting me breathe?" he whispers, his voice hoarse. Not from beating. No. My guys haven't touched him since I met Ana. No, the detox from the shit in his veins is what is killing him now. Quitting cold turkey when he's this addicted is probably not wise, but I have the doctor on my payroll checking him out and Bruno or one of the boys watches him twenty-four-seven. I figure that's more than he deserves and definitely more than I owe the fucker.

I have him chained to a cable like a damn dog. On his wrist is a tight cuff that's attached to a steel chain. The chain connects to a link that's on a steel cable. It allows him leeway to walk to a bed and then to a bathroom that contains nothing but a toilet and small shower. He has no shirt on, but his jeans are starting to look extremely dirty. In truth, he looks like hell, but he's still breathing. You would think that'd make the douche thankful. *I guess not.*

"Ana," I tell him and watch as shock slams through him. That describes it perfectly. It hits him with the force of a fist to the gut.

"How do you know about Ana?"

"You've been too high to notice before, Stevens, but I know everything. What I can't figure out is how someone as beautiful and giving as Ana shares the same fucking blood as a parasite like you."

"Oh yes. Saint Ana. Let's all take a minute to bow at her feet. If we're lucky, she might spare a minute to turn her nose up at us."

His words turn me cold as I hear them. I don't think about it. I grab the fucker by the neck, slamming him up against the wall.

"Do not say one thing against Ana. You're only alive right now because for some unknown reason to me, she cares about you. Be grateful, motherfucker."

"How did straight-laced, holier-than-thou Ana get hooked up with you?"

I apply pressure to his neck, squeezing until he can no longer take air. He brings his hands up to try and claw at me, his face turning blue. "She's been putting herself at risk to try and save your fucking ass. Something I have a feeling she's done her entire life. So do yourself a favor and do not mention Ana to me unless you can be a grateful fuck. Because I warn you, Stevens, one more bad word about my woman and I'll cut your tongue out and feed it to you. Are we clear?" He doesn't answer, but then he can't. I ease my hold just enough to allow him a breath. *"Are we clear?"* I ask again. His fear of death must be larger than I gave him credit for, because his red, splotchy face nods in agreement quickly. A pity. I think I would have enjoyed cutting out his tongue. I give him one last shove. He doesn't go anywhere because he is still against the wall, but it makes me feel better. Then, I step back.

"Why are you here?" Allen asks when he can talk again. His neck is red from where I held him and I feel a certain amount of satisfaction from seeing it.

"Since I'm letting you live, I thought it would be a good time that you and I come to an understanding, especially about your sister."

"And if I refuse? You'll kill me? You might as well do it now."

"No." I sit in a chair just beyond the reach of Allen's chains. "If you insist on being a fucking idiot, I'll do worse."

"Worse than dead?" He laughs. *Jesus Christ, he is naïve.* No wonder Ana has worried herself sick over him. She's done him no favors trying to protect him and take care of him, though. He's weak in more ways than just his penchant for sampling his own merchandise. "Good luck with that."

"Much worse," I assure him, staying on course. Today's visit is all about putting real fear into him. "I'll turn you over to Kuzma," I tell him, naming the head of the Russian mob. "I'll be sure to tell them you're the fucker who's been messing with their business in town."

He pales, and I know my barb hits home. Even he's not that stupid.

"He'll just kill me too. Either way, I'm dead."

Apparently he is that stupid. Again, I'm amazed that he and Ana share the same blood in their veins.

"He'll make you pray for death and eventually he will kill you. It's what he does from the time he has you until he grants your prayer that you need to worry about."

"What do you want from me?" Allen asks after a few minutes of silence.

"Just your cooperation. Well, that and some information."

"About what?" he asks, hate shining in his eyes.

"Ana."

He gets this weird look on his face, but he nods his head in agreement. *Finally.*

28
Roman

It's been a fucking day. I wish I had just stayed in bed with Ana. I left her brother and it's official. *I can't stand the motherfucker.* That's the only conclusion I've come to. His constant disrespect of Ana tests my limits continually. I get the feeling he's holding something back from me, something he's enjoying keeping a secret. I have no idea what it is. I wanted insight into Ana. I thought I'd be able to get more personal information from her brother than what my men would have found. I just can't figure out exactly what cards Allen is holding—*or thinks he is.* Something about that man sets every alarm bell I have off. I'm going to have Bruno dig deeper into Ana's background. If she's hiding something, I need to know what it is.

The day got worse after dealing with him and I wouldn't have thought that was possible. I traveled to the Ocean View Nursing Facility to visit Reese's mom. I lost two good men thanks to that fucking stunt pulled by Paul Banks. That fucker is a thorn in my side and I've been putting off dealing with him. He's a cop, but as crooked as the day is long. I should know; he used to be on my payroll. The thing is, most of the men I have on my payroll I can trust. There's honor involved, honor among thieves if you must. Paul Banks has *no* fucking honor. He didn't feel he was getting a big enough cut and the motherfucker mishandled a deal I was involved in, so I cut him loose. Problem is, Paul didn't take to being fired and left out of the payoff. I could give two shits about it, except now he's morphed into super-cop, determined to bring me down. I would have already killed the motherfucker, but I was trying not to draw attention to myself while brokering a deal with Kuzma, but my patience is near an end. Telling a wife her husband wouldn't be coming home yesterday was bad. Today, telling Reese's mom that her son is dead was worse. He's all she had. I'm taking over all of her bills and she'll never have to worry about anything for the rest of her life, but that means shit when it comes to never seeing her son again.

I'm walking down the hall to go outside when I hear a woman screaming. At first I tune it out. Hell, if I was in this place and unable to get out, I'd probably be screaming too. I walk by the door of the room in question. Hearing some woman call another person every vile name they can think of, and all I can think is, *I need out of this place.*

That's when I hear her. *Ana.*

"Mom, I told you I can't get you out of here. I have to work fulltime. There's no way I can take care of you."

"Bullshit. It's your fault I'm in here! Get me the fuck out of here! I'll go live with your brother, Allen."

"That'd be great mom, except no one can find the asshole," Ana says with a huff.

"I don't give a fuck what you have to do, Ana Louise Stevens, you get me the fuck out of here. You owe me that much."

"Mom, I can't," Ana argues. The distress in her voice is so thick, I find myself walking into the room before I can even think about it. Ana has her back to me. She's talking to an older woman across from her who sits at one of those table-on-wheels. "You're fine here," Ana continues, walking around the table to her. She begins putting an afghan around the woman's obviously useless legs. "They take good care of you. With my job, there's no way I can…"

I see it happening, but there's just no way I can stop it. The woman screams loudly and slaps Ana hard across the side of the face. The sound of flesh hitting flesh echoes in the room followed by Ana's pain-filled gasp. I don't think. I take the few steps that are necessary to get in front of Ana and look at the shrew in question. Her hand is half raised to strike Ana again. I grab it by the wrist.

"Lady, if you lay so much as one more finger on Ana, it will be the last thing you do," I warn her coldly.

"Who the fuck are you?" the bitch barks at me, trying to yank her hand away. *Not happening.*

"Roman!" Ana gasps. I lift my eyes to her and the angry telltale hand mark has already bloomed on her face.

"Ana, go to my car."

"Roman, that's my mother, I can deal with her."

"I said go to the fucking car, Ana."

"Jesus, is *this* the man you're fucking?" the woman growls.

"Mom," Ana starts.

"Now, pet."

"*Yes, now, Ana,*" her mother mimics, and I'm starting to see where Ana's brother gets his charm. Thank fuck my woman seems to have skipped that particular family trait. "Has he taught you to fetch too?"

That's it. No more. "Ana, Robert is waiting by the limo. Go and get in it now," I growl and the command in my voice is one I've not really used with Ana before, and perhaps that's been wrong. She looks at me, her eyes round. The anger and coldness in my voice isn't directed at her, but there's no way for her to know that. Truthfully, I am upset with her and she will know that later, but I want to shut her bitch of a mother down first, then I'll deal with Ana.

"Limo? Well, la-de-dah. No wonder she's fucking you. All that money and you are leaving me in this hellhole? You fucking cunt," her mother hisses the vile words. Ana's body physically jerks from the verbal blow. Then I see this steel mask lock into place. She doesn't even look like the woman I know.

"Maybe if you had stopped shooting up and snorting, you wouldn't have to be in here and I wouldn't be working my ass off to make sure there are people to wipe your ass because you left your body too broken to do it yourself," Ana says, her voice monotone and as cold as I've ever managed to make mine.

Her fucking mother starts to respond, and that's when I tighten my hand on her wrist enough that I know the woman feels the pain. I could break it with just the slightest movement either way. It wouldn't take much because the woman is a bag of bones. I've never in my life threatened violence against a woman before, but in this case, I think I could gladly make an exception. Jesus Christ, what kind of fucking hell has my woman lived through?

"Ana," I warn her, not wanting her to hear what I'm about to tell her mom, but also needing her to mind me for motherfucking once. Her hand goes to my shoulder, her touch trying to soothe me. *It does not.* Then, she leans up to kiss my cheek.

"I'll be by the limo," she whispers near my ear.

"Not by the limo, Ana. Inside it."

She stops when she gets to the door. "Yes, Roman," she says before leaving. Now if I could just teach her to say those words all the time, my life would be fucking simple again. I give Ana a few minutes to get gone. Her mother is strangely quiet. I let go of her hand and step away from her, the bitch stinking up my air.

"You don't look like a man that has to pay for pussy. Especially worthless pussy like my daughter's."

"If you want to remain breathing, you'll shut your fucking mouth. Do you know who I am?" I ask her. Most people in Miami do, but then most people aren't locked up in a long-term nursing facility.

"Why the fuck would I?" she hisses. She reaches for her cigarettes on the table. It's then that I notice one of her hands doesn't work. Actually, it seems like most of that entire side doesn't work. I don't know what happened to her, but from what Ana said before she left, I imagine drugs. I hate fucking junkies. It's why I don't deal with the shit. I leave that to Kuzma. The drugs are the only reservation I have about getting into business with him. Being in business with them however, means less headaches for me and added firepower. It makes damn good money sense. It keeps me being the only stop along the coastline for gambling and women. Not to mention, it gives me more firepower to protect what's mine and to protect the women in my stable. There's always some motherfucker out there thinking he can take what's mine, always trying to steal my business. That's not about to fucking happen, but I'm having to defend that shit so often, having Kuzma's firepower, not to mention police protection would solve a million problems.

The first item on my list is fucking ending Paul Banks. I'll be doing it either way, but being certain there would be no legal backlash would be great. I don't need all of the law enforcement agencies in Miami and Federal people looking at me with a fucking target on my head.

I grab the bitch's cigarettes from her fumbling hands. Taking one out and handing it to her, I keep the pack in my hand, taking the lighter too. Maybe she's starting to wise up, or maybe she just really wants that cigarette, but I sense the change in her. I have her complete attention now.

"I own Miami. When I say I own it, I mean this shithole you're living in too. It will look like fucking heaven compared to what I can do to you. You're a miserable fuck, I get that. You are probably like your fucking son and would rather die than keep drawing breath. What you need to realize is, there's much worse things than dying, and I can make sure you find that out firsthand."

"What the hell are you talking about?" she asks, but I hear the nervousness in her voice; I see her eyes and how they are dilated.

"You like drugs. I have friends use this stuff on their enemies that, with one injection, turns you into a vegetable. When I say that, I mean you will be fully alert, fully awake, but hooked to a machine that feeds you, have diapers on your ass, and not be able to bitch about how miserable you are. Unable to move. It's bad shit. I've never been tempted to deal with it. That is, until I saw a miserable bitch raise a hand to my woman."

"Ana is—"

"My property. Mine. No one touches what's mine, least of all you. Your hand, your words, your breath no long touch my woman. If I hear it does, I promise you, you'll find out firsthand what living in real hell feels like."

"You're bluffing."

"You think? Ask around. I guarantee people here know who Roman Anthes is, even if you're too stupid to. You don't want me as an enemy, woman, but that's too late for you. Much too late. If Ana comes back, you best be a fucking saint ready to kiss her fucking feet. And believe me lady, I'll have eyes on you from here on out."

The bitch wisely doesn't say another word. I smash her cigarettes up in my hand. The smell of tobacco fills the air around me. I make sure there's not one motherfucker in the pack that can still be used before letting them fall to her lap, then I walk to the door.

"Don't try me on this bitch," I warn her on my way out. "I've never had much taste for harming a woman, but after what I've just seen, I'd make an exception for you, and I'd fucking enjoy every minute of it." With that, I toss the lighter across the room, having it land on the floor a few feet from her. Then I leave. Time to deal with Ana next. Thank fuck that will be more enjoyable than the other shit I've dealt with today.

29

Ana

I'm walking slowly from the building, keeping my tears at bay and trying to keep from running from the nursing home. I fucking hate dealing with my mother. *I hate it.* It brings back too many ugly memories, too many things I've spent my life trying to hide from. The last thing in the world that I wanted was for Roman to witness my shame.

And my mother is my shame. She always has been. I hate her. I despise her and yet I can never seem to turn my back on her. I force myself to visit her once a month. If I went more than that, I'd probably be one of those people about to jump off a ledge they used to send my unit out on sometimes. Dealing with her makes me feel that desperate. It makes me feel that *stupid.* How can I still feel any type of responsibility or loyalty towards someone who doesn't deserve it? Someone who was high my entire childhood, passed out, or in emergency rooms from overdosing? Someone who let drug addicts and johns into the same house she kept a twelve-year-old girl and a nine-year-old boy while she worked out her next high?

Roman wasn't wrong. There's a reason I sleep with a gun under my pillow. A big reason, and it has nothing to do with being a cop. It has more to do with a frightened little girl and boy hiding in a closet scared the latest monster would be worse than the one before. It has more to do with the last time a fucking asshole thought it was okay to try and rape a sixteen-year-old girl. One man stopped him: Paul Banks. He took me out of the hellhole, set my brother and me in county care, and took an interest in seeing me succeed. I tried to get Allen to follow me, but I think the memories haunted him more. I'm not sure. He turned to the same shit that helped make our life miserable to begin with. There are days I can't forgive him for that. I'm so lost in my thoughts, I jump when Robert touches my shoulder.

"Go ahead and get inside, Ms. Stevens," he says, surprising me.

"Ana," I tell him, and my voice is thick with unshed tears.

"Ana," he says gently. Maybe he can sense how close I am to breaking.

I get into the limo and look out the far window, lost in memories I've spent a lifetime trying to forget. I'm so deep in them I almost didn't notice Roman opening the door and sliding in beside me, pushing me further on the seat. It takes him all of two minutes to grab me and haul me back on his lap. His arms go around me and his heat slowly melts into my body as I relax against him, burying my head in his chest.

"I know I told you to do nothing today and rest. To wait for me to get some business done so I could help you move to the house."

"I needed to visit the sea creature."

"The sea creature?"

"Vanessa. The womb donor from hell. Everyone always call her Nessie. She was more terrifying than the loch ness monster growing up. So Allen and I took to calling her the sea creature."

"Let me guess. You and your brother were into Sci-Fi when you were younger?"

"We had a neighbor, Mrs. Lancaster. She loved old movies. We'd sneak over there when mom was out and watch television and Mrs. Lancaster would feed us. It was fun. I still watch the movies today with a smile."

"What happened to Mrs. Lancaster?"

"She passed away last year."

"A pity."

"Yeah. She has a great-granddaughter. She's working herself through school by waitressing. Mrs. Lancaster's daughter died of cancer. Life is cold sometimes, Roman," I whisper, keeping my head buried in his chest.

"That it is, pet. Let's get back to your apartment, pack up, and get you moved in to my place."

"You still want me around, even knowing what kind of branches exist in my family tree?" I ask him, only half-joking. My mother is my dirty little secret, one I've kept hidden from everyone but Paul. The only reason he knows is because of our past. I would have gladly made sure no one ever found out, especially Roman.

"Maybe because of it," he says, and I go completely tense. No. *That's not happening.*

"I don't want pity, Roman. I'm not some kid in need of rescue now. Maybe I once was, but I rescue myself now. I don't have to depend on anyone. I fought hard to get that, and I don't want you trying to swoop in and make it better for the poor charity case. That's not—"

I trail off when he grabs the side of my neck and pulls my face up until I'm looking at him.

"I'm trying to go about this gentle, pet, because you're upset."

"I'm not…"

"Don't lie to me. If the way your body is shaking doesn't give you away, the tears in your eyes do. So this is me, a man not used to putting others first, trying to be gentle with you. But I know you can feel the way my cock is hard against your ass and I think you get I want to be touching you and holding you all of the time. If not, let me spell it out for you. There's not a fucking thing about you I view with pity. I see a strong woman, a beautiful woman. I see a woman I want to fuck and dominate and lose myself in over and over. I see a woman I've claimed and one I won't give up. I see a woman who fucking fascinates me to the point that I canceled the rest of my day so I can spend most of the afternoon being gentle with her in hopes of getting between her legs without feeling guilt tonight, when I'm not so gentle."

"There's a lot there to take in," I tell him, my brain replaying his words. All of them and everything they say storms through me and they make me feel *alive*. Roman doesn't give flowery words and seduction. His words are raw. I could be lying to myself, but I think they are full of truth. I decide to give him truth in return. "What if I don't want gentle?"

"Ana."

"What if need the exact opposite of gentle from you, Roman?" His eyes literally bore into me for a minute, maybe two. Then he reaches over and pushes the button on the door.

"Yeah, boss?" Robert's voice comes over the intercom.

"Change of plans. Take us to my apartment, Robert," Roman tells him, then immediately turns the intercom off. The heated way he looks at me makes everything inside of me grow hot. "I hope you know what you're asking for, pet," he warns me.

So do I.

30
Roman

The rest of the ride is tense silence. Tense because I really want to fuck her now and not wait. The only thing that stops me is, I want her in a bed. Correction: I want her tied to the bed and at my mercy.

Somehow, I make it out of the limo and elevator without attacking her. The way she keeps looking at me, the obvious desire on her face, and the ragged breathing that makes her breasts literally dance with each breath, all combine to make that a near miss. So much so that when I turn to close the apartment door, locking us inside, I remain facing the door to calm my breathing. At this rate, it will be over way too soon and I don't want that. Ana is a flower I need to unwrap one sweet, delicate petal at a time.

"Roman?" Ana questions.

"Bedroom. Now, Ana. Lose the clothes and lie on your stomach and wait for me," I tell her without looking at her, going to the bar to grab a drink. I need to calm down, to take the edge off before I go to her. I expected her to argue, but she doesn't. Instead, she silently walks down the hall to the master suite. I watch her go, my eyes transfixed on the way her jeans hug her ass. I finish my drink and pour another one, all while barely taking my eyes off of the last place I saw Ana before she disappeared. All while imagining her on my bed naked and waiting for me, that tight ass of hers sticking up in the air. I down my second drink, not even taking the time to enjoy it. I've held back as long as I can. When I clear the doorway to the bedroom, I almost come in my fucking jeans.

I thought I was prepared, but I realize there's no way you could be prepared for this. Ana is resting on the dark purple sheets on my bed. Her milky white body, a perfect contrast. Her blonde hair is scattered across her neck and shoulders, her head turned to the side, and those violet eyes are watching me. How did I get to be the lucky son of a bitch to have her in my bed? How in the fuck did I survive before she came along? More importantly, how the fuck did I get so wrapped up in her in such a short time? All are good questions, and all of the answers to those questions don't matter one fuck. The point is, she's here now, and she's mine.

I take off my cufflinks, leaving them on the small table by the door, my eyes glued to Ana's. She swallows nervously as I loosen the tie from around my neck.

"You get that you are mine now, pet? How it displeases me if you put yourself in a situation where you could be hurt?" I ask her, walking towards the bed and wrapping the tie around both my hands, stretching it.

"I'm sorry, Roman," she whispers. I expected arguing, something.

"On your knees, Ana, and face me," I order. Her eyes go wide, but she does as I order. "Give me your hands."

My eyes could get entranced by the way her breasts sway with her movements and the puckering of her nipples as she reaches out her hands to me. Everything about Ana screams feminine and it calls to the man inside of me whose job it is to claim and protect it. I pull her hands together so the wrists touch and caress one another. I wrap my tie around the delicate area, admiring how small and perfectly contoured she is. There's not a part of her body that I don't love—not a part that I don't want to stamp my ownership on.

"Roman?" she asks, not quite knowing what she's asking, but

I understand. I read the excitement coursing through her body almost as clearly as the fear that broadcasts in her eyes. Fear. Another emotion that calls to the man inside of me. The beast that is at my core. *The need to conquer and possess.*

"Turn and face the headboard, pet," I instruct.

The delicate muscles of her throat work as she swallows and turns to do as I said. Just another thing to be fascinated over. I love everything about how her throat works when it drinking down every drop of my cum. Each time seems different, special. Will it always be that way? That's definitely something I will devote myself to learning. I take the ends of my tie and secure them to the latch I keep attached by a clasp under the mattress. It will give her limited movement, which is exactly what I want. I then start slowly unbuttoning my shirt. Our eyes are locked and the look on her face makes me feel like a King. Greedy. She's greedy for whatever comes next. For what *I* give her, next.

"You were a bad girl, Ana. You are not to leave unless I, Robert, or one of the security men who work for me knows where you're going or is with you. The fact that you snuck away from me and could have been hurt displeases me," I tell her, tossing my shirt on a chair as if I didn't have a care in the world, as if I wasn't about to explode.

"I never agreed to all of that, Roman. Besides I only went to visit my mother," she whispers, her head going down into the pillow as her breathing increases to the point I can see it shudder through her body. My hand goes under her chin and I pull her face back to look at me because I need her to see what I'm saying. I need her to know how serious I am.

"She is not a mother. You will not mention her name in our bed again. Do you understand?"

It might be unreasonable, but the woman I met today was no mother. There was nothing maternal in her body. She was a monster, and I know without even investigating further that she left scars on Ana. Scars that you might not see on the outside, but are there nonetheless.

"Roman…"

"Answer me, Ana."

"You said… 'our bed'…"

Her words make me stall for a split-second until I see the emotion in her face. Does she not realize the rules that I've broken for her? Does she not get that I'm completely obsessed with her? What could she have possibly thought I meant when I said I claimed her?

I reach out and slide my hand down her head, my fingers playing with the whisper-soft blonde tendrils. The pads of my fingers trail down the skin on the back of her neck. I smile as a shiver rakes through her as slow as a lover's caress. My hand continues along her back, leisurely traveling the plains of her body and committing it to memory. I stop when I reach her lower back. Her ass curves out, forming a perfect half-globe shape that tantalizes me. My hands move down to massage each cheek, my fingers biting into them and pulling them apart to see that small dark opening they hide.

"Do you know who owns this body, Ana?" I ask her, my tone light as if I'm talking about the weather and betraying nothing of the need inside of me. Along with my question, I continue applying pressure into one of her cheeks while I take my other hand and move lower between her legs. I take my index and middle finger and dive between the lips of her pussy, pushing and seeking until I find that swollen clit. She's soaked with need, and if I didn't have other plans, I would slide under her and let her ride my face until she smothered me in sweet cream. Instead, I drag them back through her pussy and up to that small forbidden hole in her ass. I push them inside without warning.

She squeezes down on them, trying to reject their entry, crying out. I hold her ass still with my hand and push until my fingers break free of the muscles guarding the tight opening.

"Roman!" she cries out, and my dick jumps. I feel a bead of pre-cum slide down my shaft. My balls are so full and ready to explode, they feel like lead weights.

"Who owns your body, Ana?"

"You do, Roman. God help us both, you do."

For some reason, her dramatic answer makes me smile. I slide my fingers in and out of her ass, pulling them apart to stretch her with each new entry. Ana is grinding her chest down on the bed, dragging her breasts against the silk fabric of the sheets. I take my fingers out and she whimpers when they don't go back in. I have other plans, though. I move to the side of the bed, roughly pulling her up to her knees. I hold her until she manages to steady herself on her elbows. I go back to rubbing her ass with one hand while massaging her pussy with the other. She's bucking against my hold, whimpering with need and trying to grind against my hand, thrusting towards it in uneven, completely broken thrusts. She's fueled by lust and it's beautiful—but not enough. I lean down, letting my breath fan against her side, my lips grazing her hip.

"Such a beautiful little pussy. So hungry and greedy, it's trying to devour my hand. You'd let me fuck you with my whole hand if I could get inside, wouldn't you, pet? You'd do anything I ask right now if I just let you come. Say it, Ana."

"Anything," she whispers on a heavy breath.

I take my hands away, refusing to give her any kind of relief. Instead, I bring my palm hard on her ass. My dick jerks as the noise of my hand slapping that white fleshy ass rings through the room.

"Roman!" she yells out in surprise.

I spank her again, and again. She's trying to get away, but that too is impossible, and by the time I deliver the tenth stinging slap, she's thrusting up to meet my hand and panting.

"I'll ask you again, Ana. Who owns this body?"

"You do!" she hisses.

I manhandle her. There's no other way to put it. There's nothing easy about the need slamming through me right now. I flip her over. The small area of movement she had with the tie ceases as the fabric twists and wraps around her wrists one more time, pulling taut. She cries out, but her hands are positioned high above her head, just like I want them. This won't last long, so I won't worry the pain will be too much. Later, I'll take her slower. Now, the need to be inside her has been too long denied.

I push her legs up against her chest, opening that pussy to me. It's so wet and covered in her juices, I could lose it right here. Instead, I spank the wet, juicy lips of her pussy. My dick cries as her body jerks up toward it. Her body shakes and I could swear a small orgasm runs through her body. She cries out my name and that drives me to take it further. I pull the lips of her pussy apart and slap my hand against it again, this time centering most of the attention on her hard, pulsating clit. She says something, but she's so far gone the words are unrecognizable. Cream is literally pooling from her pussy, coating the side of her thighs. If I could stand it, I'd continue doing this over and over. Right now, my cock is demanding his due.

"Who owns this body, Ana?" I demand again. I'm going overboard, I know it, but I can't stop it. My need for her to admit that she's mine is as elemental as breathing.

"You," she whimpers, her body shuddering.

I unlatch my pants, pushing them down my hips. I don't have time to undress. I'll worry about that later too. I line my cock up at her entrance, raking the head back and forth in her juices.

"I'm going to fuck you, Ana, and fill you with my cum, branding you from the inside, out."

Her head comes up to look at me, her eyes round and she's biting her lip. "Hurry," she gasps, and that's all the encouragement I need.

I brace myself on her knees, which are bent back against her body, and thrust inside her. Her muscles immediately clench my cock tight, rippling around it in a way that I know I won't be able to hold on for very long. I pull out and then thrust back inside, firm. When I'm seated deep inside of her, I grind down on her pussy. Her body shudders beneath me and she cries out my name as another orgasm pummels her body—this one much bigger. Over and over I ram in and out of her, riding her hard. I can feel the heat run through my dick and my cum releasing into her.

"After I'm done," I breathe, "I'm going to fuck you again."

"Yes. God, yes," she whimpers.

"Then, sweet Ana, I'll pull out and come all over this body," I tell her, stroking her stomach with my hand and envisioning my cum all over the creamy white skin. I'm shuddering as my climax moves through me, but I want to hold off, not give in completely until I give her the words that will show her just how obsessed I am. "I'll pull out and come all over this body," I repeat, "just so there's no fucking doubt that you are, in fact," I take a breath right before I trust back into her, "*mine*."

I give in to the demand of my climax and let stream after stream of my cum jet inside of her, painting her fucking womb with my seed. I know it and I own it. I want her pregnant. I want Ana fucking tied to me, unable to get away. I collapse to the side of her, my head on her breast. I shiver as my dick slides from her body. My hand goes to her pussy and I hold it there, holding my cum inside of her, not wanting one drop to leave her.

31

Roman's headed to the nightclub. I watch him until the elevator doors close and enjoy the dark knowing smile he wears as he watches me. I'm wearing nothing but his white buttoned-up shirt, which is too big for me. My hair is rumpled because he just fucked me to an inch within my life. My body is deliciously sore and I wish he wasn't leaving. When the doors close, I take a deep breath and fall back on the Italian leather sofa. The damn thing is so soft, it should be illegal. I close my eyes and try to get a grip on my emotions, just like I do every time Roman leaves me.

I've been living with Roman in this apartment for two weeks now. Two weeks of his constant attention and being his woman have altered me in ways I never expected. Honestly, we've settled into a routine, and if only it wasn't built on lies and deceit, I would be completely happy.

I've been ignoring Paul's summons. He's getting more insistent. Roman almost caught one of his 911 texts last night from the small prepaid cell I keep. I hid the phone in a bunch of towels and distracted him with sex. I seem to distract Roman a lot with sex.

I've been putting it off, but I'll have to touch base with Paul and I'm dreading it. He'll want to know if I've planted the coke and set up a sting. I haven't and I don't think I can. I'm just dreading the conversation with Paul.

I grab the cell from my purse and text Paul:

Cloverfield Medical Complex. 2 p.m.

Even setting up the meeting twists my gut. I'm apparently going to Roman's physician to get checked out today. He informed me it's something we should have done weeks ago, but I make him forget his rules. He's already shown me the clean bill of health the doctor gave him and I guess this is my turn. I want to be offended, but let's face it, in today's world that's smart. Probably way too late, considering we're fucking like bunnies every chance we get, but whatever. Besides, I can't hardly be offended since I'm lying to him every time I turn around.

That's starting to bother me too. They warned me you can go too deep undercover, so deep that you start to lose sight of who you are and become the person you're portraying. The thing is, in this case, I'm being me. *The real Ana.* The Ana that I've kept hidden since I was the scared sixteen year old that Paul Banks saved. When I'm with Roman, it's not about being someone I don't know; it's all about letting my guard down and showing him who I am. Which is crazy. Completely crazy.

Roman swears he's doing his best to help me with my brother. He hasn't shown me proof, but I still find myself believing him, which makes me wonder if I didn't have Roman Anthes pegged wrong to begin with. He's becoming more relaxed around me, so much so that in this past week, he's even beginning to talk business in front of me. Not a lot, but little things, enough for me to understand he's brokering a deal with the Russian mob. That should terrify me—and maybe it does— but not enough to turn me away from him.

My phone vibrates. I look at the text with a feeling of dread:

About fucking time. I'll be there.

The more I see the words, the more I want to vomit. I clear off all history of the texts and bury my phone back in my purse. I can't put this off any longer. I jump in the shower. It's a busy day and I don't have time to waste. I've got the doctor's appointment, the fight with Paul (and it will be a fight), and then tonight I'm accompanying Roman to a dinner party. He bought me the sexiest, barely-there little black dress I have ever seen. I'm all set, but I'm a nervous wreck about it, too. I may need medication to survive today. That's my last thought as I go jump in the shower.

Time to stop putting things off.

32

The doctor's appointment threw me off. I'm feeling like the world's biggest idiot. How did it not register to me that I had been having unprotected sex with Roman for two weeks? Unprotected sex with a man I've been trying to get information on to prove he's part of a Miami underground drug ring? A man I suspected at one time of killing my brother? Unprotected sex. Maybe Paul's right and my brain is all fucked up. Maybe the best thing would be to have the DEA and FEDs pull me.

I'm kicking that around in my head as I make my way to the first floor to meet Paul. My appointment was at one and I'm now ten minutes late. I texted him and told him to wait for me by the pharmacy area. There's an alcove right off the main room where I can meet with him briefly. It's the most I can chance right now. I don't think Roman has me tailed, but I'm sure he has Robert watching me and making sure I'm okay. If there's one thing I've learned about Roman Anthes, it's that he's very protective.

"You're fucking late," Paul barks at me. I look around to notice the area is empty. The pharmacy is shut down for a late lunch, so thankfully no one is around to hear him.

"Will you shut the fuck up for Christ's sake before you blow my cover?"

"You've been radio silent for two fucking weeks and you expect me to be concerned with blowing your fucking cover? What's wrong, Ana? Afraid Roman won't fuck you anymore if he knows you're a cop?"

I don't even think. I slap him across the face. The force of my hit turns his head sideways. He brings his hand up to his face and looks at me with contempt. Had my relationship with Paul not already been deteriorating, that look would have destroyed me. "Fuck you," I growl.

"Who knew sleeping with a felon would give you spunk," Paul says, his voice deadly. He brings his hand up to rub where I hit him. "Maybe once you're done playing Roman's whore, I'll give you a go so you can compare."

His words make me want to hurl. They literally make me gag. The man I looked up to and thought I owed so much to says these vile things. I thought of him as a father. My stomach cramps with the need to vomit. I breathe through it, instinctively determined not to show weakness to him.

"I want a new handler. If you don't make it happen, I will. The choice is yours," I tell him, my voice quiet. I turn to leave and he grabs my hand, pulling me around to face him.

"You think you're getting off that easy? You signed up for this fucking job and you'll tow the line or you'll pay. I've had Anthes in my sight for over a fucking year and I'm not letting some wet-behind-the-ears wanna-be-detective ruin it for me. You have until tomorrow afternoon to plant that shit, or I'll have someone else do it."

"You can't—"

"Watch me. Do your fucking job, Ana. That's why you're here. That's the only reason you're here. Don't forget for even a minute that if Anthes knew you were a cop, he'd kill you without a second thought. You're nothing to him. Nothing but an easy piece of ass who keeps her legs spread."

I start to slap him again but he grabs my hand, preventing me.

"What happened to you?" I ask confused.

"Not a fucking thing. Except a woman I used to admire has become the fuck-toy to one of the vilest men in Miami. Get your head out of your ass and back in the game, Ana. Do your job, or

I'll do it for you."

"I'm no one's fuck-toy. You're overstepping your bounds. I could have you—"

"What the fuck is going on here?" Roman snarls. My face goes pale as I turn away from Paul to see Roman standing at the door.

Fuck.

33
Roman

The last thing I expected to see was Ana standing there yelling at the one man I'm dying to kill. *Paul Banks.* If there's a man more deserving to be on the wrong end of a pistol, I haven't met him. Which is saying something, in my line of work. My eyes narrow on the hold he has on Ana and the strange look on her face. I walk to them, anger fueling every step. There will be no saving the motherfucker now.

"I suggest you let go of my woman, Banks. *Now*, while you still have a hand."

Paul turns her loose with a look of disgust. "Anthes. I didn't realize they let scum out on the streets this early."

"What the fuck is going on here? Ana, how do you know this weasel?" I ask, and her face blanches and goes even whiter.

"Ana and I go way back. I never figured you were one to take my leftovers, Roman. I guess you're growing bored of sampling the women who work for you."

I hear Ana's gasp, but my attention has turned to the fucker in front of me. *All* of my attention is on Banks.

"Ana, go to the car," I order.

"Roman, he's lying. I never slept with him."

"To the car, Ana," I tell her again, showing no emotion, but I'd be a fucking liar if I didn't admit to the fact that knowing she hadn't been with Banks doesn't soothe something inside of me. "Robert, escort Ana to the car," I tell my driver. I don't turn to make sure my order is followed. I know it will be, and I don't trust Banks enough to take my eyes off of him. "You come near Ana again, and you'll regret it."

"Has the mighty Roman Anthes fallen for a pussy?"

"You heard me, Banks. You can push your weight around all you want, but you and I both know what a bottom dweller you are. Be careful you don't end up at the bottom of an ocean."

"Is that a threat, Anthes? Threatening cops can get you in deep shit these days," he responds arrogantly.

"Not a threat. I don't waste my time with threats. I'm saying you so much as sniff the wind in Ana's direction and I'll end you. Take that any way you want."

"Maybe she's the one sniffing in my direction. Trying to find a real man who—"

I strike out before he can finish, my knuckles crunching against his teeth. He goes down with a thud. Blood pours from his lip and I hope I've at least knocked his teeth loose.

"Ana is not on your radar. *Ever.* Consider this the only warning you'll get, Banks. You might hide behind your badge, but don't forget I know where you've fucking buried the bodies."

It's a useless warning. He signed his death warrant when he put his hand on Ana. I planned on ending him for a while; I was just holding off, not wanting to draw possible attention as long as I was talking to Kuzma, but some things a man can't ignore.

I walk away from Banks then, pulling my phone out and calling Bruno. "Banks has overstepped for the last time. You got the number of that guy we used near Orange County? Marcum?"

"Yeah."

"Call him. I want this fucker handled. Set up a meeting tomorrow. I have that damn charity dinner tonight."

"You got it, boss."

I click the phone off and walk out towards the limo. I need to find out from Ana what the fuck is really going on because I don't believe for a minute she's let Banks between her legs. I hope like hell I'm not fucking lying to myself.

34

Ugly. What just went on brought new meaning to the word "ugly". I'm still trying to wrap my head around it. The bad vibes Paul gave me when trying to force my hand the other day at my apartment were bad, but I didn't think they'd go this far south. I never expected Paul to morph into someone I did not know. Someone I don't *want* to know.

I'll have to think about it later. What I need to worry about the most is Roman. What the hell am I supposed to do now? *What did he hear?* I don't think I'm going to be able to distract him with sex this time.

Time for questions are over when Roman slides into the limo like a dark thundercloud.

"Roman …"

"How do you know Banks?"

"Roman. I—"

"Answer the question, Ana, and do us both a favor and don't lie to me," he growls.

His tone and words take me aback. I want to scream at him, but I can't. It would be ridiculous, considering I've yet to tell him the entire truth since I met him.

"He saved me once."

Roman's face grows harder. "Saved you how?"

"I don't want to talk about that."

"Too fucking bad. Tell me, Ana."

"Fuck you!" I growl before I can stop myself. I've had enough. Enough of men putting pressure on me. Enough of this war going on inside of me, enough of everything.

"Fuck me?" he asks, seemingly astonished, and maybe he is. I doubt any woman has ever told him to go fuck himself before. Roman's probably got a long line of women who are ready and willing to say yes.

"You heard me. I've had it with men telling me what to do! That includes you, *Daddy!*" I punch the intercom button. "Robert, pull over."

Roman's eyes narrow and he pushes the button a second after me. "Robert, if you pull over, you're fired. Take us to the apartment."

"You can't keep me here."

"I can fucking do whatever I want."

"Fine! I'll jump out!"

I'm acting unreasonable. I'm just so freaking close to my breaking point. I can still feel Paul's hand gripping mine and hear his hateful words. I feel like I've lost someone dear, because *he's dead to me.* The Paul I thought I had in my life obviously doesn't exist anymore. I don't even get to grieve that before Roman is upon me with his demands. I just can't handle it. Not right now. I need to get away…

"The fuck you will," Roman growls, pulling me onto his lap, but there's nothing loving about him this time. His grip and hold is hard. His arms are like a prison, locking me into him. I try to pull away, twisting and turning, bracing my hands on his shoulders to push away from him. His hand wraps in my hair and knots in it. I pull, ignoring the pain. It's useless. He's not letting me move. He pulls my head up and I'm trapped, not only by his hold on me, but by the look in his eyes. "You're going nowhere, Ana. *Ever.*"

His words should fill me with fear. *Instead it's excitement.*

35

Roman

I know I'm being irrational. I haven't been able to be rational about this whole thing since seeing Ana with the one man I despise above all others. Seeing his hand on her and touching what is mine only made that feeling more intense. I'm charging at her instead of giving her time to talk and be rational. But being rational is beyond me right now. I'm one step away from the ledge and Ana is trying to push me over. I've been gentle with Ana. *Way too gentle.* In a way, today is my fault too. She forgot who is in control. *Time to fucking remind her.*

"I want to know how Banks *saved* you."

"And I don't want to tell you!" she growls.

I'm a dominating man. It's elemental to who I am. Until Ana, that's been relatively easy. Women fall in line effortlessly. Ana's continued defiance alternates between driving me insane and exciting me.

I claim her mouth. Our lips collide with so much energy there is almost pain. Teeth clash and our tongues war. My hand is tight in her hair, holding her, forcing her to submit while I devour her. I bite into her lip, not enough to break the skin, but enough to get her attention, leave signs I was there, and to show her who is in charge.

"How do you know Banks, pet?" Her eyes are spitting fire at me. Her tongue is moving over her swollen lip, trying to brush away the sting. "Ana," I warn, almost at the end of my rope.

"He was a beat cop that was called out to my mom's when I was sixteen. One of her customers woke up and, since mom was passed out, he thought he'd give me a go."

Her words are hurled at me and they wound, as they were meant to. I pull tighter on her hair, not because she's displeased me, but because her words light something inside that makes me want to kill. And I will. I will hunt the motherfucker down and kill him. I don't care that's it's been over ten years. His blood will be on my hands and I will be the reason he draws his last breath. "Did he…?" *Fuck, I can't even say the words.*

"No. Paul stopped him in time." I refuse to feel an ounce of gratitude to that fucker. It's not in me. "Until recently, I thought Paul was a friend. I looked at him like a father."

I ignore the fact that she viewed a man my age, maybe a couple years younger as a father. I might be too old for Ana, but I'm not giving her up. Something else bothers me about what she said, however.

"Until recently? Have you seen Paul before today?"

"Until today, I meant. I'm sorry I'm just so rattled. He hates you Roman. Why does he hate you so much?"

She sounds frightened, and if she really cared about Banks that much, this had to be a hard blow for her, yet here I am, holding her. As guilt hits me, I let go of the stronghold I have on her hair and pull her into me, holding her close in my lap. I absently brush her hair with my fingers as I try to figure out how to put the things I need to say without hurting her further.

"You get that what I do might not be something everyone could handle. I deal with rules and laws outside of normal society."

"Roman," she starts, but I shut her down.

"It's just facts, pet. I'm not asking you to condone what I do. I'm not asking for absolution. In fact, I love the fuck out of my life and things I do. It's who I am. But some people might view me as slime, as the dregs of society. If I'm that, then Paul is worse. He has no honor even towards the laws in my world. He's a bottom dweller, pure and simple, and the world would be a much better place if he had a bullet put in him."

Her body tenses up and she tries to pull away. I know that I let my hate for Banks overrule my tongue. I didn't go softly, not even a little bit.

"But Roman, he's a cop. He's devoted his life to—"

"This ain't the movies, pet. Good guys don't always wear white. Some of the lowest fucking men I've dealt with hide behind a badge."

"You sound like you hate cops, but they keep the world from chaos. Without laws…"

I put my hand on her neck and pull her eyes to me. She needs to get this. I need her to understand. My world is the world she resides in now. She's not leaving, so she needs to accept who I am—*what* I am.

"Men, pet. Men are human. There are good and bad in all of us, and I abide by my laws. It keeps chaos in my world from getting out of control and that world is yours now."

"Roman, I'm not sure I want to be in your…"

I stop the words with a kiss, drinking from her lips in a kiss that's sweeter and gentler than any we've shared before. Our lips move against each other, caressing. I suck her bottom lip into my mouth, pulling it with my teeth and running my tongue along the inside curve. Slowly, her mouth opens, the warmth and taste of her invading me and drugging my senses. My tongue moves in, seeking hers and dancing with it, trying to convey how I feel about her without the words. Words just get in the way. Ana and I have always communicated best through our bodies.

When the kiss is finished, she pulls back slowly, curls into me, and rests her head against my shoulder. Her arm goes around me and she holds onto me. It's a simple gesture, but one I will never take for granted. Nothing about Ana being mine, can be taken for granted.

"Take me home, Roman," she whispers.

Home. I haven't had one of those before Ana. She's home for me. I wrap my arms around her and settle back into the seat, counting the minutes until I can make love to her.

Make love.

36

Ana

It might sound stupid. Maybe I'm the stupidest woman in the world. But when Roman pulls me in his arms and he kisses me... when all of this powerful, strong, and virile man's attention is centered on me, I cave. I know what kind of man he is. I know what he's done in his life. I've read page after page of all of the things that the DEA and FBI know Roman Anthes has done, but can't get proof. So, maybe I am crazy. All I know is that I feel loved, cared for, and safer in Roman's arms than I did standing near Paul today. Paul was the one who scared me and seemed out of control. Going with Roman and being with him felt... *right*. There's no other way to put it.

Nothing about this case has turned out the way I thought it would in my head. Nothing I thought about Roman Anthes jives with the man I'm slowly falling in love with. I'm losing sight of my purpose. I'm supposed to be trying to save my brother. I'm supposed to be getting proof against Roman. I'm not sure I can do that now. I don't think I *want* to do that now. And my brother, he hates me. He hates that I've kept stepping in and trying to save him. He hates that I became a cop. There's so much bad blood between us, but I can't sit by and let him die. If there's a chance he's out there and I can save him, I have to do it.

When the limo comes to a stop, I can't make myself leave Roman's lap. It doesn't matter anyway because he holds me tighter and carries me from the limo. We don't talk in the elevator either. I reach up and link my hands behind his neck and rest in his hold. It's been a day and I'm emotionally spent. I don't think I can take any more tonight. I will think about everything tomorrow. I will try my best to clear my head and plan then. For tonight, I'm going to get lost in Roman.

He carries me straight into our bedroom, placing me gently on the bed. He crouches down in front of me, pulling me around so my feet are on the ground and slides my shoes off. Once he's done with that, he cups my neck and strokes his thumb across my cheek, a move so familiar that I've come to crave it, producing a feeling that I feel down in my soul. "I'll be back, pet," he tells me, and I have to smile. I still hate that damn nickname, but when he says it with that smile, I want him to say it again and again. This magic he works on me defies explanation.

He disappears into the bathroom and I flop back on the bed and breathe for the first time since Roman saw me talking to Paul. I have this urge to tell Roman everything. How would he react? It would feel good to come clean. I think what Roman and I have is real. He'd understand.

Roman comes back in before I completely convince myself. I need to think about it. What I'm contemplating has a lot of repercussions, least of all compromising my future as a cop and, ultimately, detective. I thought that was what I wanted, but now I'm not so sure.

"Stand up, pet."

I look up to see Roman reaching for me. My hand goes in his and he pulls me from the bed. He turns me so my back is to him. The sound of the zipper on my dress sliding down is the only noise in the room. It seems unnaturally loud. His hands encircle my neck from behind. My pulse automatically jumps and a tight ball of desire curls in my stomach. He brushes his hands down my shoulders on each side, snagging my dress as he goes. The dress slides down my arms and cool air hits my chest as it falls to a puddle at my feet. I swallow because, as many times as I've been with Roman, this feels momentous. I don't know what the shift is between us, but it's there. He kisses the back of my neck at the base of my spine as his hands come around my sides to meet at my stomach. They fan out, following the line of my hips. His lips continue to leave a trail of kisses down the vertebrae on my back to the point that I know he's on his knees behind me. The idea of Roman Anthes on his knees while worshipping my body runs a giddy thrill of pure joy through me. It settles in my heart. It cements there, taking up residence.

This is real, what Roman and I have. This can't be all about sex. It feels too *different*.

When I feel his teeth bite into my hip, a moan of pleasure escapes my lips. I turn so I can look down at him. He's captured my thong in his mouth and pulls it down from my body, his dark eyes watching me the entire time. My heart beats triple the speed in my chest and every feminine part of my body clenches, preparing for an explosion. *This man is lethal.* He unhooks my garter, slowly rolling my stocking down one leg. I brace myself on the bed as he lifts my foot and removes it before starting on my other one. Each touch, each fleeting kiss grabs hold of me, refusing to let me go.

By the time he's done, I'm completely naked and facing the bed, which seems to be his plan because he stands up behind me. I feel his hot breath graze across my skin. His hands hold my upper arms against my body and he places a kiss on my shoulder, his tongue tracing my collarbone. When he reaches my neck, I automatically tilt it to the right, giving him better access. His tongue paints a path from my shoulder to my ear and back down. Then I feel his teeth bite gently into my neck, capturing the vein that is throbbing crazily, betraying my excitement. He sucks that into his mouth while his teeth knead the skin and my knees go weak.

"Stretch out over the bed, Ana," he orders.

His voice causes tremors of excitement to run through my body. I do as he asks, trying to control my breathing. He walks around to the other side of the bed and I look up at the man who is slowly owning my soul. He's holding his tie in his hand. He has this look on his face that if I wasn't already on fire for him, I would be with just that look. I reach my hands out to him, expecting him to tie them again, even wanting it. I love the feeling I get when I am completely at his mercy.

"No, pet. This evening's lesson is all about feeding your senses," he tells me.

He takes the tie and secures it around my eyes, tying it. I'm immediately enclosed in darkness. The silk material glides against my closed eyelids and I breathe heavily, wondering just what comes next.

I go a few minutes without Roman's touch. For a bit, it feels like he left the room. The heady energy that is uniquely Roman is gone. Then I hear his footsteps. It sounds like he is pacing around the three sides of the bed, and I can almost feel his gaze on me. With each minute that passes like this, my anticipation wars with my nerves. I start to smell the faint scent of cherry in the air. After a minute or two, it gets stronger.

"Roman?" I finally question, using my elbows to support me and lifting my lower half off the bed, trying to search for him blindly.

"Which sense do you think is stronger, pet? Sight? But then you don't have that one right now, do you?" he asks me. I jump because, from his voice, it appears he is standing right in front of me. "Maybe it's hearing. Do my movements sound louder to you now that you can't see, Ana?" he asks, his voice almost casual, but I can hear the undertone of need in it.

"Yes," I whisper. That's when I hear the crinkle of his slacks in front of me and feel his breath skate against my forehead as he places a soft kiss there.

"Maybe it's taste," he whispers, his voice wickedly soft.

His finger trails down my jawline, following my chin. I'm completely taken by surprise when I feel another hand hold my breast, pinching my nipple between his large fingers and pulling. When I cry out, his finger moves from my chin to my mouth, sliding inside. I close my lips around it, sucking his finger inside my mouth and sliding my tongue around it, imagining it is his cock.

He pulls on my nipple again and his lips are by my ear. "I'll definitely give you something to taste soon, Ana," he tells me, and when he takes his finger away, I bite my lip to keep from begging him to give it to me now.

I whimper in disappointment as I hear him stand up. He walks around the bed and I can hear him behind me. I try to decipher the noises he makes, but my breathing is too ragged, my heartbeat too loud.

"I think maybe touch could be the strongest sense to experience," he says, his hand moving over my ass cheeks and up to my back.

I thrust my ass back towards him, begging without words for him to take me. Instead, I feel something slap against my ass. The sting is immediate as the cold leather connects, once, twice… three times. Burning heat zips through my skin and I cry out from the force of it. My wet pussy clenches internally as more juices rush forth. I'm on a razor's edge and a breath away from climaxing. I feel something tickle across the heated skin in a zigzag type of movement. *Feathers?*

"Do you like that, pet?"

"Roman," I gasp, the blood rushing through my ears.

Just like that, the feeling is gone. Then I feel the leather return, moving across my ass in much the same pattern, but it doesn't stop. It moves lower and with purpose until it's sliding against the lips of my pussy. When it pushes into the wet valley, I moan at the intrusion. It moves as if being guided, and the hard leather rubs over my clit—back and forth, ending in a small circle, and then repeating, over and over until my ass is pushing off of the bed and my pussy is trying hopelessly to latch onto the torture device so I can at least ride it.

"Oh, pet, you are soaked. I don't think you've ever been this wet before," he says before walking away. I cry out over the loss of both him and whatever he used to spank me with. My body grinds against the mattress and my fingers bite into the comforter on the bed so tightly, I'm surprised it doesn't rip. I'm terrified he will leave me like this and not finish me off. "Hold still, Ana," he growls. I definitely hear desire heavy in his voice now. My body instantly stills as if he controls it by invisible wires. "Good girl," he says, his hand brushing along my ass, which still feels heated. He rubs it gently and then moves up my lower back. "How about we try a different kind of touch this time, Ana?"

I'm confused, but before I can ask him anything, I feel hot liquid drip onto my back. It's painful, but there's a warmth that spreads through me. It brings out an elemental response in me that's even more pleasurable than when he spanks me.

"Fuck…" I whisper as another drop hits and runs down my side.

"We'll get to that soon too, Ana," he whispers. "*Very* soon."

I watch as the wax drips down on Ana's body, gathering in deep pools of maroon and then slowly hardening as her body cools it down. I watch in fascination as the wax makes color trails against her milky white skin. Ana is so receptive to anything I do. I never thought I'd be someone who decided to keep a woman permanently, but I'm going to. They'll have to pry Ana out of my dead hands before I let her go. I put the candle down, not because I'm not enjoying the fuck out of our game, but because my dick is so hard, I can't spend another moment outside of her. I reach under her stomach and pull her up on her knees.

"Hurry, Roman," she whispers.

"Is my pet hungry to be fucked?" I ask her, my hand moving over her ass and up her back. I love touching her. I love watching the way my dark hand stands out against her pale skin. I let my finger trail over the hard ridge of the wax on her body. Satisfaction rolls through me. I love knowing that I'm seeing a part of her that no other fucker will ever have.

"Yes. God, yes," she pants.

I unzip my pants. I don't have the time to take them off. I need inside her more than I need my next breath. I push them out of my way and line my cock up with her pussy, pushing just the tip inside her. She's so wet and hungry, that's all it really takes. If I let her, she'd suck my dick in and this would end way too quickly. I take back control, holding my cock tight, trying to hold back my own orgasm. *I'm that ready to blow.* I use it to circle her pussy. Her juices are so thick, they instantly start dripping down my cock, coating me in… *her*. That possessive feeling overtakes me again and I know there's no way I'm going to be able to hold back. I slide my cock back and forth against her pussy, letting the shaft graze her clit. The lips of her sweet cunt hold me in place as I let her ride my dick like that. It feels fucking good and I can feel the way she's already trembling against my cock. My hands bite into her hips as I close my eyes and enjoy the way her slick, wet pussy moves up and down my shaft, branding it in her desire.

"I'm close, Roman," she says, her voice hoarse and full of need.

I pull back, lining my cock up. I grab her hair in my hand and pull it roughly back. "Who do you belong to Ana?" I growl.

"Roman," she cries, but I pull harder, her head coming back further as I lean over her, the hunter towering over his prey.

"Who do you belong to?" I growl, asking again.

"You, Roman. I belong to you," she whispers.

Hearing the words I needed most, I thrust into her, not stopping until my balls are pushing against the outside of her pussy. Her walls close in on my dick, squeezing and fluttering all around it, signaling how close she is. I keep my hold on her hair as I pull out and then thrust back in. I fuck her harder and harder in a way that I know she'll feel me for weeks to come, in a way that with every step she takes, she'll ache and miss my cock at the same time.

"You're mine, Ana. I'm never letting you go. Mine," I growl, using her hair to pull her head to the side and exposing her neck. I bite into her shoulder, not even thinking twice about it. I want my mark on her. I want to brandher skin with *me*.

Ana cries out and her body shakes as her climax rips through her. She meets every thrust I give her, her ass pushing back into me. I'm doing my best to hold back, wanting this to last longer.

"Come with me, Roman, please. Come with me," she whispers, the effort to form the words causing her voice to shudder.

Hearing her plead like that makes me know I'm a goner. I surrender to Ana, to everything she is and everything we are together. I may have marked her, but she marked me too, and though this mark might not be seen, it's so fucking deep that I know she will always be there.

She owns me too.

38
Roman

"Roman, you didn't use condoms," Ana says.

I've pulled us up vertical on the bed, but that is as much as I've managed. Fuck, I still have my pants on, though admittedly they are gathered about mid-thigh. Ana is on my shoulder, her back to me.

"We haven't been using those since the day on your balcony, pet. Kind of late to worry about it now."

"A baby would be a big mistake right now."

I've been actively trying to get her pregnant and I can't even put into words how much I disagree with her. In compromise, I don't comment. I kiss the mark I left on her shoulder and change the subject. "Are you hungry?"

"Not really."

"Ana? What's on your mind?"

"It's just been a long day, Roman, and I…"

"What?" I ask, something in her tone alerting me to the fact that I'm not going to like her next words.

"Roman? Do you know where my brother is?"

My body goes completely still. How did I not see this coming? Motherfucker, Banks had enough time with her to fuck shit up after all.

"Why do you ask me that, Ana?"

"'Why' doesn't matter, Roman. I'm asking you to tell me the truth. Are you the one responsible for my brother missing?"

"The 'why' *does* matter, Ana. I'm asking you to tell me where you heard it and I want to know now."

She takes a deep breath, so deep I can see it move through her

151

body, and then exhales with a whoosh as she moves to her back. Her eyes find mine and there's something in those violet depths I've not seen before and it worries me.

"The DEA have a file on you, Roman. They suspect you are working with the Russian Drug Cartel. They have photos of my brother in your club the night he disappeared talking to a man they identify as one of your security men. So, I'm asking you, Roman. Do you have my brother, or worse, did you have him killed?"

She asks me these questions while pulling away and sitting up. Anger drums in my veins along with a healthy dose of fear. I haven't felt that emotion in a very long time, but I feel it now. I can't let go of Ana. I will not lose her. Not now.

I growl, getting out of bed and pulling my pants up and securing the button to hold them in place. "Did Banks give you all that info?" Her head goes down and I don't like that shit at all. She will not hide from me. "Ana. Eyes, now." She slowly raises her head to me and the tears in them is enough to almost completely undo me.

"Is it true, Roman? Do you have my brother? Is he... dead?"

I could lie. The inclination is to do that. Ana would never know and I'd make damn sure that Banks never got near her again to talk to her. That might have been the wisest plan of action. It's also the one that would allow her to escape me. I can't allow that. I'm not letting her go.

So I revert back to what my original plan was all along, the plan my stupid brain concocted after I first saw that picture of Ana. Use her brother to gain what I want: *her.* The only thing that has changed is that the stakes are higher now. I don't want her in my bed for a week or two. I want her there forever.

"I have your brother, Ana."

Her gasp fills the room and genuine shock fills her face. She grabs the sheet, pulling it over her body. That one simple movement speaks volumes and it pisses me off.

I rip the sheet from her, throwing it to the floor. "You don't get to do that, Ana. You don't get to cover your body from me. Whatever else is going on, you gave yourself to me. You don't get to take that back."

"You lied to me, Roman! I asked you for help in finding my brother! If I mattered at all to you, you would have been honest with me."

"What would I have said, Ana? Your brother was selling drugs in my club and pissing off the wrong people and jeopardizing my business. He had to be handled."

"Was he? Oh, God... Did you kill Allen? Answer me, Roman!"

"No, Ana. I didn't kill him. I was going to, but then I saw a picture of this new dancer that had been asking questions to the wrong people..."

"Oh my God."

"And I decided I wanted her. So he's still breathing, pet. Rest easy."

"*Who are you?*"

"The man you just begged to fuck you. That same exact man."

"Everything they said is true. You are a monster."

I can't hear this shit from Ana. I'm used to being judged and I don't give a fuck, but I can't hear it from her.

"Think what you want to, pet, but you're still mine and you're not fucking going anywhere."

She gets up from the bed, finding the sheet I threw down and wrapping herself up in it again. Her eyes are spitting fire at me.

I must, in fact, be the monster she accuses me of, because I am hard as a rock.

"You can't keep me here against my will, Roman. If I want to leave, I will."

"Feel free, pet. But if you walk out of that fucking door, then I'll have no reason to keep your brother breathing."

It's a low blow and sounds so much worse now than it did when I originally came up with the idea, but I'm not about to back down, even when she pales and looks at me with nothing but hate.

"How can you do this?" she asks, tears slowly falling from her eyes.

"You can have the rest of the night to make up your mind, Ana."

"What? Where are you going?"

"Out, but never fear, pet. As long as you're in this house, your brother is safe," I tell her, turning away from her.

Fuck. This was not how I planned my evening out. It gives me one more reason to kill Paul Banks. That shit will be put into action tonight.

39
Roman

I handled that badly. Fuck. I know I did, but I was blindsided and pissed that she was trying to hide from me. The trouble with being gone on a woman is you react with your dick and not your brain. If I handled my business like this, I'd be broke.

"You look like you lost your best friend. Want me to buy you a beer to cry in?"

"Fuck you," I tell him, not looking up from my whiskey. "You're traveling late, Marcum."

"I got a call from this bastard in Miami. Sounded serious, so I thought I'd come see him."

"Dangerous, in your line of work."

"Life's fucking boring without a little danger," Marcum says. I turn to look at him. He hasn't changed much. A little gray around the edges, a few more scars, He's got long hair that he has pulled back in a clasp at the back of his neck right now. He's wearing jeans, his leather club cut, and cowboy boots. I respect the man. We might be different as night and day on the outside, but on the inside where it counts, we could be fucking twins.

"How's the fifteen kids?" I ask him, and he gives me the one finger salute. If you can say anything about Marcum, it's that he's a fertile son of a bitch. He has so many kids, he could populate a small country with nothing but his offspring.

"Eight, asshole. And not bad. Even got a grandkid now. Max's woman Tess had a little girl. Prettiest little thing you've ever seen."

"Hard to picture you as a grandfather," I tell him honestly.

"I'm fucking awesome at it. Hell, should have tried it sooner.

Lot easier than your own kids, that's for fuck sure."

"I wouldn't know," I tell him, taking a drink of my whiskey.

"That job you wanted, that's not going to be easy, asshole. That fucker has connections," Marcum says, switching to business quickly, which is just as well since I'm not really in the fucking mood for small talk.

"I'm not paying for easy. While we're on the subject, I have another problem that needs to be dealt with."

"Jesus, you're a needy fucker all at once. What brought on all this shit?"

"A woman," I growl, pouring more whiskey into my glass.

"Say no more. Jesus, brother. Shouldn't you have learned from my mistakes?"

"She's a good one, Marcum. She just comes with a fucking load of baggage."

"Don't they all," he sighs.

"Trouble with Cherry?" I ask him, mentioning his latest squeeze. He's kept this one the longest and she seems to care about him, but then what the fuck do I know about anything.

"Cherry left."

"What the fuck for?"

"Now that's the question. Unfortunately, it's a question I have no fucking answer for."

"Life would be fucking simpler if you could just keep them tied to the bed all the time," I growl, draining the last of my drink.

Marcum stands up and slaps me on the back with a laugh. "Amen, brother. Amen. I got your order in. Get Bruno to send me the particulars on your add-on."

"Will do. Where you headed?"

"Anywhere my dick takes me, brother. Anywhere my dick takes me."

I shake my head and let him go. I'd like to think he's a miserable fuck, but the truth is, I'm being led by my dick too, and at least Marcum's will have a warm place to spend the night. Thoughts of Ana in our room covering her body from me with tears running down her face flash through my head.

Fuck.

40
Ana

I pull myself out of bed. I think I'm still in shock and I didn't sleep at all last night. Mostly, I lay in bed reliving the confrontation with Roman. I thought I was prepared. I mean the DEA doesn't send you undercover for nothing. I knew all along there was a chance that Roman did in fact have Allen, but after meeting him and the way we became with each other, it just didn't seem to fit. How can someone be so good to you, be sweet and loving, and all the while be holding your brother to use against you—or worse, holding him to kill him? What does it say about me that I slept with this man?

God, what does it say about me that I miss him even now?

My emotions are all over the place and I can't seem to get them in order. My mind keeps going back to the hostility between Paul and Roman. There's more there than I know, much more than Paul will ever tell me. The man he makes Roman out to be, the man in the file the DEA has is not the man I've come to love—sorry, to *care* about.

Roman has always treated me like I mattered. Then again, how well do I know him? I jumped in head first, led by a quest to learn more about my brother—and by hormones. *Definitely by hormones.* I need to see Allen. If I can see him, then maybe things will seem clearer.

It takes me a few minutes to get dressed, brush my teeth, and look like I haven't lain awake all night crying. I'm not sure I fully succeed. By the time I've finished, Roman still hasn't shown. For all I know, he could still be gone. The thought of him spending the night somewhere else hurts me. Not because I think he went to another woman, it's just... I want him with me. *Even now*. God, I am messed up.

I walk through to the main room. Roman is sitting on the sofa, his clothes wrinkled, his hair a mess, and there's an afghan thrown over the sofa as if he slept there. It's stupid, but thinking that he has, somehow makes me feel better.

He looks up at me when I stop by the sofa. There's a look in his dark eyes... a heated look, and I fight against its pull.

"Have you decided, Ana?"

"I want to see Allen."

"I can arrange that, after I have your word that you'll stay."

"This is crazy. Do you realize you're blackmailing me into—"

"Call it what you want. Your word. I want your word."

"Fine. I'll stay," I tell him, my stomach churning. I don't know what I'm going to do, but I do know I have to stay either way... for now.

"I'll have my lawyer draw up the contract."

"Contract?" I ask, confused.

"You don't think I'm going to take you at your word, do you, Ana?"

"Roman, I don't have a law degree, but I'm pretty sure contracts built on blackmail are useless."

"You'd be surprised what money can do."

"Money and the right crook for an attorney," I tell him, unable to believe he's serious about any of this.

"Whatever, it won't be an issue, because you will stay."

"Roman, I think maybe..."

I stop when he gets up and comes to stand in front of me. His hand goes to my neck and he pulls my face up to him.

"You gave yourself to me, Ana. I told you I claimed you. Maybe you don't understand exactly what that means, but you should." His fingers trail down my neck, pulling my shirt loose and smiling. I know he sees the dark bruise that he left there when he bit me last night. Just remembering it makes a shudder of need vibrate through me. I know Roman doesn't miss it when his lips graze my ear. "You can fight it, pet, but your body knows who it belongs to. It craves me even now."

I fight against the lure of him. It would be so easy to give in, to lose myself in him. I can't. I need to keep my head straight. I should have been doing that a long time ago. I try to pull away, but Roman tightens his hold on me. "Roman, I want…"

"I bet if I touched you right now your pussy would be soaked for me."

"Roman…"

"Am I right, Ana?"

He is. I can't tell him that. I refuse to tell him that.

"I want to see Allen now," I tell him, my voice monotone, and it takes everything I have to hold my body rigid and sound like I'm unaffected. I know he can tell it's a lie, but it makes me feel marginally better. His eyes lock with mine and I see disappointment on his face as clear as day for just a split second and then it's gone.

"Fine. Grab your coat. It's chilly outside."

I take a breath and step away from him. I wasn't sure he would give in this easily. Now, if I can just make Allen listen to me without blowing my cover.

41

Ana

I follow Roman down the stairs to where he's holding Allen. Each step I take, the nerves of the unknown increases. Roman and I haven't said a word to each other since we left the apartment. I'm not sure why he's not talking, but I have nothing to say. I'm feeling so lost. In such a short time, Roman has become this rock on which I lean. I've never had that in my life, not really, and Roman filled a void I didn't know I had.

We make it down a hall to a large cemented area. Even the walls are concrete. The doors are made of steel just like the ones you would find in prison. Roman has the guard unlock the padlock so we can go inside. A part of me wants to run and hide, but instead, I force my feet to move forward. I see Allen. He's lying on the bed, his right hand chained to a cable that runs across the room, allowing him to go from the bed to a small bath area. My stomach churns because it's basically a large dog-run, except the cable is longer and more extensive.

"How did I know it wouldn't be long before you showed up, sister dearest?" he says, and the guilt hits me again. Allen is three years younger than me. I was a kid myself, but he didn't fare as well as I did with mom's boyfriends. He blames me. I didn't protect him enough. I didn't take care of him. I tried, but I obviously failed and that has done nothing but make him hate me.

"I'm sorry, Allen. I didn't know," I whisper lamely.

"Yeah. You seem to not know a lot of shit when you should. Kind of like your boyfriend. Right, sister dear? Imagine my surprise when Roman didn't know that you were a…"

"Allen," I yell, trying to stop him before he can reveal to Roman that I'm a cop.

"What a selfish bitch you are."

"That's enough, Stevens. I told you to show respect when you talk about your sister. That goes double for when you're talking *to* her. She's the only reason you're still breathing," Roman says from behind me, causing me to jump.

I look over my shoulder at him. He's standing completely still looking at Allen with hate and anger. He's doing it again, taking up for me when no one ever has before. That funny feeling in the pit of my stomach I get when Roman is around picks up. How can I not be drawn to this man? I touch his arm gently, turning into him. "Can I talk to him alone, Roman? Please?"

The one simple gesture catches Roman by surprise. I read it in his eyes. Seeing the state that Allen is in is jarring at first, until I realize one thing: *Allen's not high.* I can't remember the last time I've seen him where his eyes weren't glazed over and he didn't have that crazed look he gets when he's coming down off his last high. I don't know what exactly Roman's endgame is, but I do know right now that he's helping Allen. Call me stupid a million times—but that's what I see here, and I think Roman's doing it for me. Maybe Roman senses the way I'm softening, because he bends down and kisses my forehead.

"I'll be right outside, pet."

"Thank you."

"Pet. Isn't that precious," Allen sneers after Roman leaves the room. "Boy, if he only knew the real you, right sis?"

"What's going on with Roman and I is none of your concern."

"Wait? Are you really slumming it with the biggest criminal in Miami? Gee, I bet your boss loves that. I've already gathered

Anthes doesn't know what you do for a living. I take it your boss doesn't know about your dating activities either."

My heart speeds up like crazy. What if Roman can hear what is said in the room? I try to change the subject. "You're looking better."

"I'm looking sober. That's what you really mean, right Ana?"

"Okay, fine. You look like you haven't been high in a while."

"I've told you a hundred times, that's *my* fucking business."

"Allen, you're throwing away your life."

"You don't live with the memories I have, or the scars, Ana. When you do, you can talk to me about staying sober. Until then, just shut the fuck up."

"If you could stay sober, there are things we could do to help you cope, Allen. If you let me in, just a little bit, I'll make sure you have help. I promise."

"There you go, my goody-two-shoes big sister trying to save me. You don't seem to get it that I don't want to be saved. I never asked for your help and I sure as hell don't want it. You better tend to your own life because trust me, when Anthes finds out that you're double-crossing him, there will be hell to pay."

"Allen, he might be…"

"Listening? Do you think I give a fuck? The only reason I haven't ratted you out yet is because I enjoy watching you squirm. You've been too fucking high and mighty for too long. It's nice to poke at you. If you're wondering, I do plan to tell him soon. So you might want to find a rock to hide under."

I wait for Roman to come in, demanding to know what we're talking about. When nothing happens, I breathe a little easier. "Are you not even going to listen to me?"

"Nope."

That's when I give up all hope of ever reaching my brother. I knew it was a longshot, but I had hoped … Hell, I'm not even sure what I hoped. For something more than this, that much is clear. "Will you... will you at least keep my cover until I can manage to get you out of here?"

"Are you working on that?"

"Paul is."

"Great. The DEA. So I'll be trading this cage in for a new one. No fucking thanks."

"Allen, they have you for dealing meth and coke. You have to know there's not much I can do. My hands are tied. But I'll be here for you, and by taking this assignment, they've told me they'll make sure you get treatment. You can still live a good life, Allen. We both can. You just need to hold on and help me stay under the radar for a little longer."

"Tell you what, sis. I'm feeling generous. You have forty-eight hours. After that, I'm singing like the caged canary I am."

"Allen, I only want to help you. If you'll just let me try and..."

"You should leave before I decide I'm being too agreeable."

"I love you, Allen." He doesn't answer, but then I didn't expect him to.

This seems so useless now. Why did I think this might be Allen's rock-bottom? Why did I think he would accept my help now? Maybe I am as stupid as he keeps telling me I am. This is just one more thing to add to everything that's been going on. I feel like a small fish being surrounded by sharks and completely out of my depth. I give up and leave because that's all I can do. There's more I want to say, but there's truly no point. Too bad I didn't realize that before I begged Paul to let me go undercover.

42
Roman

When Ana comes outside, she looks so heartbroken that I want to strangle her brother's neck. I walk over to her and pick her up in my arms.

"Roman," she gasps, but I ignore her. She's mine. I might not be able to protect her from pain, but I can damn sure try to minimalize it. "Will you let me down? I can walk."

"Shut it, Ana," I growl.

Having her in my arms and feeling her ass pushing into my skin again, that's what I needed. Last night was the longest fucking night of my life. I'm not giving her room to get free of me. I was stupid to even allow that. She stays tense in my arms during the whole time it takes to get her back to the limo. When I slide inside, Ana still in my arms, I can feel tension leave her. It soothes over some of my anger. She lets her guard down when it's just the two of us. I like that because fuck if that's not when I feel alive. If I had no one else in my life for the rest of my years but Ana, I'd be perfectly okay with that. Fuck, I've even decided to back out of the deal with Kuzma. He'll still do his business, but it will just be away from my club. In return I'll make sure my club is clean so he doesn't have competition. It works better for me and it keeps that shit away. The things I deal with might be illegal as fuck, but gambling and whores don't usually have the blowback drugs and guns have. I want Ana pregnant with my child. I don't want that shit touching her or our baby.

"He's so angry," she whispers, and it's then I notice my shirt is wet with her tears. I hold her close.

"What's his story?" I ask her.

I don't really give a damn, but seeing the dynamics between the two, I know there has to be something between them. I find myself changing from wanting to kill the fucking kid to trying to fix him. For Ana. *Always for Ana.* I've already accepted that this is my reality. I may never have planned on claiming a woman, but she's mine and by God I will move Heaven and Earth just to make sure she doesn't cry like she's doing right now. I keep rubbing my hand back and forth on her arm, kissing the top of her head and just holding her close while quiet sobs shake her body. The interior of the limo is alive with her sadness. It's killing me, but all I can do is let her cry it out.

"Remember how I told you about the man who thought he'd try to turn to me instead of—?"

"Shh... Ana, I remember," I tell her, not wanting her to repeat it, not wanting to ever hear about it again. I had Bruno track down the fucker who was arrested in the police raid that Banks was a part of. I sent the information to Marcum. He's gone. I made his head top priority. I can deal with Banks breathing air a few more days. The thought of the fucker who tried to hurt Ana drawing more breath is unacceptable. *Completely unacceptable.*

"I wasn't his first choice. That night... wasn't the first time it had happened," she whispers the guilty secret.

"Ana?"

"I ran and hid," she whispers remorsefully. "God, Roman. Paul doesn't believe me, but I didn't think he would. I mean I know now I was naïve, but Allen was a boy. A little boy. What kind of sick monster would... *Oh, God.*"

"Ana, sweetheart..."

"I hid in a closet, not knowing that just a room over that monster was raping my little brother," she confesses, crying. "When... when Allen finally told me, it had been going on for a week, Roman. *A week.*"

"What did you do when you found out, pet?"

"I tried to…"

"What, Ana?" Knowing what she's about to say, the hate burning in my gut is threatening to explode.

"I tried to—" She breaks off, unable to say the words. Her face is buried so tight into my chest that her words are muffled. No one should live with the misery that my woman has locked inside of her. How did she get to be such a giving person? How did she rise above everything that is in her past? More reasons that Ana will always fascinate me.

"You tried to sacrifice yourself to save your brother, didn't you, Ana? That's when Banks found you."

"Yes."

"Ana, sweetheart, you did all you could do. You were just a kid."

"Allen was younger. I should have protected him more. I should have known that a monster preys on all children, not just one because she's a girl. I was stupid."

"You were a kid. That's all, Ana. Just a kid. If anyone is to blame, it's that snake whose bills you're paying in that nursing home."

"Allen despises me most of all for that. But I couldn't just turn her out on the street, Roman. I hate her for what she's done. But she can't even go to the bathroom by herself. I can't just turn my back…"

She can and she should, but that's a fight for another time and if I have to pay room and board for that bitch the rest of her life, I will, but my woman will never see the woman again. I won't allow her poison anywhere near Ana.

"I know it may not feel like it, Ana. But it will be okay. I'll make it okay."

"Some things even the great Roman Anthes can't accomplish," she half laughs, half cries.

"Watch and see, pet. For you, I can do anything," I tell her truthfully, making a mental note to call Marcum again. There's going to be a slight change in plans.

"Are we not fighting anymore?" Ana asks.

The question makes me go tense for a second. "Are you still mad at me?"

"No. You've been trying to get Allen clean. Haven't you, Roman?"

"I would have killed him, Ana. You saved his life, but I can't lie to you. People don't cross me without me making an example of them. That's who I am."

"Can we forget about who you are outside of the time you're with me and the same with me? Can we just be Roman and Ana when we're together?"

"Ana, I'm keeping you. That means the outside stuff will always be there. We can't bury our heads in the sand and expect—"

"I don't mean forever, Roman. I mean just a few days. Please? Give me a few days to just have you." *Just have you...* I love those words, and for once, Ana and I are in complete agreement.

"Then let's go back to my house. I have some engagements coming up. We'll spend our time there and enjoy the beach."

"Your maid hates me, Roman."

"She's paid help, Ana. I'll make sure she knows you are in charge, if she plans to keep working for me."

"Whatever you want," she whispers, her voice sounding very tired.

I relax back into the seat, Ana still in my lap. It's not but just a few minutes later her breathing evens out and I know she's sleeping. I gently maneuver to get my phone out while not waking her up—not an easy task. I punch the number in.

"Yeah?"

"Change of plans. I want the package delivered to me."

"That's a lot of bread. I'm not in the curbside delivery business."

"Money…"

"Is not an object. I get it. Did I mention the fact that you're a needy fucker?"

"Later," I tell him, not commenting.

"Later," he agrees and hangs up. With that done, I hit the intercom to tell Robert to just drive me straight to my house. I have a new wardrobe there for Ana, and anything I need will be there too. I suddenly don't want to wait one more minute to get her out of this damn car.

43
Ana

"Roman?" I moan, waking up. When he doesn't answer, I look around the bed to find I'm alone. I glance at the clock and notice it's a little after midnight. Stretching, I get up, wanting to immediately find him.

We've been back at his house for two days, two days that have truly been the best in my life, two days that I truly needed. Seeing Allen almost killed me. Since being undercover, I've been pulled into a million different directions. I feel like I've lost myself. And maybe going back to Roman's house and hiding out is running away, but I don't care. I know things will come to a head with Paul and his crew—and probably very soon. Hell, my brother will be the one to tell Roman before Paul even gets a chance. So, I'm going to take what time I have with Roman and enjoy it. Maybe I can make him so happy that when the truth comes out, he'll not care. He'll know I was... Jesus, what was I? In love with him, while setting him up to go to jail?

I love Roman. That revelation makes my heart physically hurt and drum erratically in my chest. I love Roman. I push the thought back before I give myself a mini heart attack. My hand goes to my stomach, resting there. I have so many secrets. *So many.* I just don't know how to get out from under them.

I wrap the sheet around my naked body, taking a breath. I pad quietly down the hall, searching out Roman, but careful not to make too much noise. If there's one dark spot on my time spent here, it would be Mayra, Roman's maid. He made it clear to her that I am, in fact, her boss now. You would think that would change her attitude towards me. It has, but only in front of

Roman. When it's just me and her, there are waves of hate coming off of her. If I weren't keeping a million secrets, all of which will blow up in my face soon, I'd call her on it. As it is, right now, I don't feel I have the right.

"Roman?" I whisper again, this time at his office. I turn the knob and see him sitting there at his desk talking on his phone. His hair is rumpled and he's wearing slacks and nothing else— and he looks sexy as hell. Roman has a tattoo on his chest. It's the only mark he has. It says: "Strength and loyalty". It's beautiful and I want to lick it every time I see it, even if lately the word "loyalty" makes me feel horrible. Roman deserves my loyalty. He's never done one thing to hurt me. He's not the man I read about. That's the thing. When I took this case, he was words in a file, a means to an end, a criminal. Roman is not that person to me now. Whatever happens, I know beyond the shadow of a doubt that I can't continue this line of work because, if anything, it has taught me that sometimes the bad guys aren't all that bad, and the good guys can be rotten to the core.

Roman motions me inside, but I hesitate. "I'll just go back to our…"

"Sit, pet," he orders while cupping his hand over the receiver of the phone. He's smiling. But then, he's been smiling a lot in the two days we've been here. I'm proud of each one because it feels like I gave that to him. When I start to walk around to the front of the sofa and sit, he stops me. "On the back of the sofa, Ana. Sit facing me so I can see you."

His command sends ripples of desire through me. Which, after the workout he gave me earlier, should be impossible. I sit on the back of the sofa, feeling weird. Roman gets up, all while still talking on the phone about some deal overseas. I'm not really listening; I'm entranced with the look in his eyes.

He comes to a stop in front of me and adjusts the sheet so it gathers at my hips, leaving the entire top part of my body exposed. My nipples tighten and pebble as the cool air hits them. Roman bends down and moves his lips over one, and then the other. I whimper at the feel of his tongue brushing against them. He centers in on my right breast, using his tongue to bathe it, flicking back and forth along the nipple slowly and methodically. Moisture pools between my legs, painting the insides of my thighs. I bury my fingers in his hair, needing more of him. He sucks the nipple in his mouth and I gasp loudly, my pussy quivering. He releases it, blowing against my breast with his heated breath. My eyes close at the sensations he evokes. When I feel his mouth on my nipple again, I thought I knew what to expect, but then he bites it—and not gently. He does it in a way that the pain washes through me and makes my whole body quake because I know with Roman, that sting of pain means more pleasure than I could have ever dreamed before him.

I cry out his name. "Roman! Give me more, please?" I whimper.

When he rises up with a look of satisfaction on his face, I realize he's still on the phone. I bite my lip hard to keep from begging him to fuck me. Roman backs away to his chair. He sits down, watching me. I swallow against the intensity in his look.

"Maria, we'll have to finish this discussion later. Something has come up requiring my attention," he says, hanging up the phone.

"Who's Maria?" I ask, jealousy firing on all cylinders before I can stop it. Heat hits my face because I know Roman realizes my possessiveness.

"My secretary, pet."

"Is she pretty?"

"Beautiful," he says and a sick feeling twists in my stomach.

"Have you... fucked her?"

"Would it matter? I haven't touched another woman since I saw your picture, Ana. I haven't even looked at another one."

"It shouldn't matter..."

"But it does?"

"I'm sorry." I know I am being unreasonable, but I'm still wishing I could throat punch his secretary right now.

Then, Roman grins. *He grins.*

"My possessive little pet. I think I like this side of you. But it doesn't matter," he says, unzipping his pants, his eyes never leaving mine.

"It doesn't?" I ask, losing track of the conversation because I can't drag my eyes away from Roman as he takes his cock out of his pants. It's fully erect, and just seeing it makes my insides clench with need.

"No," he says, but it's his hand that has my attention. His hand is squeezing his cock and then stroking it so slowly that I swear I can see as every centimeter of his dick vanishes behind his hand. As the head disappears where I can't see it, I watch as his other hand comes out and massages his balls. His cock becomes shiny with the juice dripping down it. Everything inside of me is demanding I go to him and take him in my mouth.

"Why doesn't it matter?" I ask, my tongue coming out to lick against my bottom lip, wishing I could taste that one large drop of pre-cum that drops from the head of his cock onto his hand.

"My secretary is a happily-married great grandmother of five." My eyes move up to him at that and he's... *grinning.*

"Asshole," I grumble. I want to watch his cock again, but the joy in his smile is more captivating. I couldn't turn away from it if I wanted to. Then, he laughs. A full, *deep* laugh. If I hadn't already admitted to myself that I was in love with Roman, this would be the moment. *He's laughing.*

"You are constantly surprising me, pet," he says, and he has no idea. Yet, his words make me inwardly cringe. How surprised will he be when he finds out my *biggest* secrets?

I swallow, needing to distract myself. I don't want to think about that. Not right now. Not with Roman stroking himself and my body exposed to him.

"Roman, you're driving me crazy. I need…"

"What, pet? What do you *need*? Do you need to be fucked?"

"Yes! God, yes."

"You need me to pound that pussy, sweetheart?"

"Please, Roman, stop teasing me," I whimper. I start to slide off the sofa. I don't care if I have to crawl to him. At this point, I'd do anything—I'm *that* close to the edge.

"Don't move, Ana. Stay where you're at."

My body feels as if it weighs a thousand pounds as I brace myself on the back of the sofa again. I know Roman by now. If I disobey him, he'll torture me for hours.

"How long do I have to sit like this?" I ask him, letting my eyes go back to watching his hand move slowly back and forth on his cock.

"Until I get tired of looking at what's mine," he says simply. A statement of fact. For some reason, that makes me more excited than watching him. That makes everything in me feel like one touch from him would make me detonate into another stratosphere.

His. A simple truth.

44
Ana

"Roman," I whisper, unable to drag my eyes away from his cock.

"You're so beautiful, pet. So fucking beautiful."

I can't hold back anymore. Despite his command for the opposite, I slide off the couch and onto the floor. I crawl to him like a tiger stalking her prey. His hand stalls on his cock and I know I've surprised him.

"Ana," he starts, but his voice is gruff. My tongue comes out to lick along my lips as I watch the head of his cock and the way his pre-cum drizzles down the shaft. When I reach him, I put my hands on his knees and slide my body between his legs.

"Let me suck you," I beg, dying to just dive in and do that. I'm already going against his orders though and I want Roman to need this as much as I need to give it to him.

"Pet, always pushing me. What am I going to do with you?" he asks.

Unable to resist, I flatten my tongue against the base of his cock and lick up the throbbing vein that runs the length of his shaft, gathering his pre-cum on my tongue as I go.

"Fuck."

The need in his voice gets to me more than anything. Roman is so controlled and intense, I love pushing him and making him let go of that. I suck just the head of his cock into my mouth, humming against it, as my tongue dives in to seek more of him, needing more of his taste. His fingers tangle into my hair and I take that as approval, whether it is or not. I widen my mouth and hollow out my jaws and slowly sink down on the length of him. I don't stop until he's at the back of my throat. My hand comes up to roll his balls, kneading them. They're hard and firm and so fucking warm. Slowly, I back off his cock, keeping my lips locked tight around it so that when I release him completely, the wet popping noise echoes. His entire cock glistens now with a combination of my mouth and his own juices. I lock eyes with him, licking my lips and breathing hard, not trying to hide how excited and turned-on I am. I want him to see it.

"I love the way you feel in my mouth, Roman. I love to feel your hands tighten in my hair as you demand I take you all the way back."

"Pet…"

"Fuck my mouth, Roman. I don't want gentle. I need you to take charge," I tell him.

His fingers tighten in my hair, flexing back and forth as he watches me. "You're tempting the beast, Ana."

"Good," I say simply, lowering my head down. I slide his cock back into my mouth and Roman's fingers tighten in my hair, knotting in it. I slide down his shaft slowly, my pussy clenching, my breasts tingling, the nipples tightening with need. I feel electrically charged and so fucking turned on I might die if I don't have him. Roman reaches down, his fingers dancing across the soft skin of my breast. He kneads the skin, causing me to moan, the sound muffled and needy, barely coming out around the mouthful of cock that I'm sucking on. Roman's hand leaves my breast, traveling down my stomach and stopping at my pussy. His hand moves between my legs. Maybe I should be embarrassed by how wet I am, but I'm not. I like that he can feel how wet he makes me, how much this excites me. I lean towards him, up on my knees, trying to tempt him into moving his fingers deeper inside of me.

"You're so fucking wet, Ana. Do you want my cum, pet?"

I can't really answer him with words because my mouth is so full of his dick, but maybe he can tell by the way my desire pools around his fingers right before he thrusts them deep inside of me. He growls his approval right before he takes complete control. His hand pushes my head up and down on his cock, fucking my face hard and fast. He curls his fingers in me, hitting that mysterious spot that men before him have never even gotten close to. My orgasm pushes through me, my hand holding his balls and manipulating them as he uses me. I can feel them tighten beneath my fingers. I know he's close as I fight my gag reflex to give him anything he wants.

He pulls me off of him and I cry out at the unfairness of it. I earned his cum. It should be mine. Before I can argue, the first spray jets across my face, splashing on my lips. His hand holds my head in place as he jacks his cock, aiming for my face and shooting stream after stream on me until it's dripping down my neck, running between my breasts, and sliding down my throat.

I'm covered in... *him.*

45

"I thought you were taking the week off," Ana questions, pouting.

It should annoy me, but it does the opposite. I'm glad she doesn't want me to leave. I can't tell her why I'm leaving, even if I think this will help her brother, and though I'm doing it for her, I doubt she will understand. I don't have a lot of experience with worrying about how a woman reacts. I've never given a fuck. I have a suspicion that Ana would not be pleased with my plan, however. I lock my hand on the side of her neck and pull her face to mine. She stretches up off the mattress to meet my kiss. Just the touch of her lips soothes me.

"You'll barely notice I'm gone, pet. I'll be back by evening."

"Trust me, I'll know. Plus, you're leaving me here with Broom Hilda, the wicked witch of the..."

"I thought she was treating you better?" I ask, immediately pissed off. I warned Mayra to treat Ana with respect. Ana is a permanent fixture in my life. I'm not letting her go. I will, however, fire the maid. *Easily.*

"She is, around *you*. She waits to show me her distaste and hate when you're in another room."

"That's unacceptable. Why didn't you tell me?"

"Really, Roman. It's not a big deal," Ana says.

"It is. I told you to fire her if she kept disrespecting you," I complain, upset this has been going on without my notice.

"She's been better. I'm rarely alone with her. Besides, it doesn't matter. I'll deal with her. It won't be long until..." she trails off as her face heats up.

I think about what she said, and any way I choose to finish her sentence displeases me.

"Until *what*, Ana?" I growl this time, my voice dark.

"Roman, let's not get into this right now. You'll be late," Ana says, refusing to meet my eyes.

She's right, I will be. I don't give a fuck. Something about hearing the woman you are obsessed with talk as if your time with her is limited has a strange effect on a man.

"Ana, we've gone over this shit. Do you not get that I'm not letting you go?"

"Roman..." she trails off for a second, her eyes looking down at her hands instead of me.

"Ana. Eyes, now," I order, and her face snaps up and her eyes sparkle with displeasure, but fuck that, she needs to understand this. "You are going nowhere."

At my words, some of the anger leaves her, but there's another look on her face now, one I'm not sure how I feel about. It almost looks like *hopelessness.*

"Let's just take it one day at a time, Roman. If I'm still around in a month, I'll handle her..."

"Mayra!" I yell, my voice loud enough to shake the rafters in the ceiling. I've had enough of this shit. Ana must know because she pulls away, jumping at my tone. She pulls the sheet tight around her body and now there's fear in her eyes. My dick pushes against my jeans because caring for Ana or not, I'm still a bastard. The sight of her fear makes me want to control and conquer her that much more.

"Mr. Anthes?" Mayra says from the door. I turn to watch her freeze as her eyes go to Ana lying in my bed. Her dislike shows on her face clearly before she hides it and raises her eyes to mine.

"I told you, if you didn't respect my woman, you were finished. Apparently you didn't take that to heart."

"I have no idea what you're talking about, Mr. Anthes."

"Ana says you've been disrespecting her in private."

"Roman," Ana starts, but I ignore her. The controlled mask on Mayra's face slips somewhat.

"I've been doing my job, Mr. Anthes. I don't have time to cater to the whims of some—"

"My woman. That's who she is, Mayra. She's mine. She's staying. I will have my ring on her hand and my child in her belly. She will be around for a long fucking time. A lot longer than you will."

"Roman," Ana gasps.

"Mr. Anthes," Mayra starts. I ignore them both and instead pull off my jacket.

"Pack your things, Mayra. I want you out of this house in thirty minutes. Robert will drive you back into town. I'll mail your severance pay. I'll be generous though; it's more than you deserve."

"You can't be serious!" Mayra protests, her face now full of hate, but now it's not all directed at Ana.

"Deadly, and now you have three less minutes to pack than you did before."

"Bastard!" Mayra spits at me. I grin. She looks at me, and then back at Ana. "You'll regret it," she snarls and then stomps out. I grab my phone and call the security detail that is on duty in the guardhouse by the gate to my estate.

"I've just released Mayra Baxter from employ. She has thirty minutes to leave. Have Robert waiting on her and a man on her as she walks from the house to the limo please."

"Got it sir," I hear right before I hang up. Ana is sitting up in bed, her face full of shock.

"Roman, I don't think... I mean... Why would you... What are you doing?" she stutters before finally getting the only question that matters out.

"I can't leave until Mayra is gone," I tell her, unbuttoning my shirt. Ana's eye watch my every movement.

"About that, there's still time. Maybe you could talk to her and get her... Roman! What are you doing?" she asks again, her back going straight as I unzip my pants.

"You have thirty minutes to make me forget."

"Make you forget what?" she asks as I kick off my shoes and discard the rest of my clothes. When I'm completely naked, I walk to the other side of the bed. My dick is hard and leaning towards her. Bastard knows what he wants.

"That you thought for one minute you were leaving me," I tell her.

"Roman."

"Shut it, Ana," I tell her. I palm my dick, stroking it once, slow and hard. I pull her on the bed by her leg until she's lying crosswise. She doesn't fight me; I think she's still in a sort of shock. "Spread your legs wide, Ana." I order.

She hesitates for just a second, and then slowly opens her legs wide, bracing her feet on the mattress. Her pussy is glistening. *Perfect.* I line up with her entrance and slam home, not even bothering with gentle. I don't have that in me right now.

"Mine!" I growl like a fucking caveman. Ana's arms go around me, her nails biting into my back as she stretches to find my ear so I can hear her moan of approval—and then her whisper.

"Yours, Roman. I'm yours," she reassures me. The words calm the beast inside of me. *For now.*

46
Ana

I watch from the window in the study while the lights of the limousine disappear. Watching him leave fills me with a feeling of doom. Is today the beginning of the end? He said he had to go to work, not to visit my brother, but would he tell me if he was? He promised he was just going to help him get completely sober and then he would let him go. What Allen did from there on out would be up to him.

But Roman probably won't get that chance.

I'm sure Paul is working overtime on ways to set Roman up, especially since I have been MIA and ignoring his phone calls. Just the thought of that man and what he could be up to causes fear to fill me. I turn cold, fine sweat breaking out over my body. I've begged Roman to be careful and warned him that Paul will be looking to bring him down. I've even taken to searching the house and the limo, just in case whoever else Paul has on the inside might try to plant what I wouldn't. I've not found evidence of anything going on, but that doesn't do a lot to make me feel better. I wrap my arms around myself, my thoughts somehow chilling the whole room, unease filling me. I need to do something.

"Do you need anything, Ms. Stevens?" One of the security guys that Roman has on staff asks me. I forget his name, but then there are so many people working for Roman, there's no way to keep them all straight.

"I'm fine. Thanks. I was just about to lie down. I seemed to have developed a headache," I lie.

"Fine. If you need anything, you can hit the number zero on

the phone. That will call security."

"Thank you," I tell him, watching as he leaves the room.

Once he does, I count to ten. Then I worry that's not enough and count to ten again. Panic fills me and I worry it's still not enough. By the time I've counted enough times to hit fifty, I figure I need to quit stalling. I move over to the fake ferns that are in the entry way planter along with multicolored flowers. They were so lifelike, I thought they were real—until I touched them. I guess when you have enough money, even fake flowers can look better than real ones. It takes me a little bit of digging because I buried the phone well, not wanting anyone to find it. Once I wrap my hand around it, I breathe a little easier. I get it and then start looking towards the back of the planter for the battery. It takes a few minutes to find it and then I walk to the sofa and sit down with the newly assembled phone. I stare at it a minute before turning it on. Then I dial Paul's number and wait. It doesn't take long—two rings.

"About fucking time. What the fuck are you doing at Anthe's house? You know what the fucking plan is."

"How did you know where I was?"

"Don't be completely stupid, Ana. Did you carry out your orders?"

"No, Paul. I need to talk to you. I think—" I would argue more, but the phone goes dead. That's when the fear really hits. I swallow against the bile rising in my throat. It's time for me to either come clean with my superiors and hope they are more trustworthy than Paul, or come clean with Roman. Either choice is bad. There's no guarantee that my captain will even listen, and given the choice, I know the majority of the team members will back Paul over Roman, who they view as scum. To them, they'd just be getting another perp off the streets. Telling Roman means warning him and betraying my badge—and it also means admitting to Roman that I've been lying to him since day one.

Damned if I do, damned if I don't. Either choice is going to be hell.

The house phone rings and I jump. I shut my phone back down. I don't take the battery out of it again, however. There's no point. Paul knows where I'm at, and it's clear he's not about to try and contact me now. I reach over and grab the telephone and, reading Roman's cell number on the caller I.D., I go ahead and answer it.

"Hey," I whisper, hoping he can't hear the worry and panic in my voice.

"Pet, there's a business dinner tonight. I've tried to get out of it, but there's no way. It begins at seven."

"Oh, okay," I tell him, a little disappointed. "What time will you be home?"

"Be home? Ana, you will be going to the dinner with me. There's a blue dress in your closet that I picked out personally. Put it on, and wear your hair down—I don't like it when you wear it up. I'll talk to you later."

He hangs up just like that, and I stare at the phone wondering what the hell just happened. My worry over everything going on with Paul and Roman takes a back seat as I replay the conversation in which Roman doesn't ask if I want to go to a dinner; he just demands it, then instructs me on what to wear and how to fix my hair. Anger takes the place of worry. The asshole just expects me to fall in line like everyone else in his life. I decide to concentrate on him being an asshole and not on the impending doom that's breathing down my neck. I'll make up my mind on whether I should come clean with Roman or the detective in charge of the investigation tomorrow.

Tonight, I have a lesson to teach Roman Anthes.

"Who the fuck is this?"

I watch as Ana's brother looks at the fucker that Bruno just threw down at the man's feet. The bastard in question is hogtied. He couldn't move if he wanted to. Marcum really is a master when it comes to ropes. He's got a gag in his mouth and the bruises on his naked body and face tell me that this was a job that Marcum enjoyed.

"He doesn't look familiar?" I ask Ana's brother.

You can see the exact moment recognition hits him. Allen's body literally shakes with it. Then he goes pale, so motherfucking pale I'm starting to think the son of a bitch is going to pass out in front of me. Slowly, I see the heat of anger replace every other emotion.

"Ana fucking told you?" he screams. "That fucking cunt had no right! Get him out of here, you all fucking need to just get out of here. Kill me already! Stop torturing me! Who the fuck do you think you are? I can't…"

I stop his tirade by grabbing him by the neck and slamming him hard against the wall. I squeeze his neck so tight, his face begins to turn blue. His hands don't even come up to defend himself. Then I look into eyes, eyes so much like Ana's that it's unreal. Except these eyes are full of an emotion I never want to see in Ana's: *misery*. The son of a bitch truly wants to die. It's time for some hard truths and it seems I've been elected to deliver them.

"Not one more fucking word about Ana. The reason you're alive right now, motherfucker, is because of Ana. The reason I'm giving you even a ghost of a chance is because of Ana. For some fucking reason, she loves you. She believes in you. I'm a selfish asshole, so I have to tell you. If you were anyone besides her brother, her even caring for you would be the end of you. Instead, I'm giving you someone to take your aggression out on. I get you're fucked up in the head. I had to hear my woman cry. She's innocent to the slime in this world. She hasn't been exposed to the shit we have. You and I know how fucking twisted shit is. Ana doesn't. A frightened girl ran and hid from a bastard not knowing her brother would even be considered a victim. You get that? She didn't know." I see the need to argue with me in his eyes. I let off the pressure on his neck slightly— not enough for him to talk and argue, but enough so he can breathe. "What you don't know is that once she knew, she tried to get the monster's attention away from you. She tried to sacrifice herself to keep him from going after you again. What you don't know is that she blames herself every fucking day. So you need to get your head out of your ass. Focus your anger on this bastard until you can start to breathe clear again."

"What do you know about anything?"

"A fuck of a lot more than I'll ever tell you."

I see indecision in Allen. I let Allen stew in everything while I instruct the boys to untie our plaything and chain him up on the wall.

"What's it matter? I go to jail. I don't have anything to live for anyways. Just fucking end me and stop torturing me. Word on the street was, you don't let people breathe air that cross you. Jesus, why are you putting me through this shit?? *End me already!*" Allen says, screaming his last command, his whole body shaking from the force of it.

That's when it hits me. *Full-on. In the fucking face.*

"You picked my club because you had a death wish. That's

why you ignored my warnings. That's why you kept coming back, even knowing you were getting on the Russian's radar?"

The kid shrugs, but avoids my eyes. "I figured between you and Kuzma..." he says, but doesn't finish the thought.

"If you wanted to die so fucking bad, why not just eat a bullet?"

"Because no matter how bad I wanted to end it, I could never pull the fucking trigger! *There!* Satisfied?"

"What if I told you I had enough power to keep you out of jail?" Allen's face jerks up to me. Disbelief is clear, but there's something else.

"Why would you be willing to do that?"

"Because you matter to Ana." I tell him the truth. I've come to the conclusion I'd do anything for Ana. Absolutely anything. Even save her worthless brother. Though, if I want to think about it, I can admit to seeing a little more in him now. Maybe something even worth saving.

"You're that gone over my sister?" he asks while I take off my jacket and lay it over the top of a chair. Ana is something I'm not discussing with Allen. Something I'm not discussing with *any* motherfucker. I motion to Bruno and he tosses me the baseball bat I brought earlier.

"You gonna help me end this motherfucker or not?" I ask him, gripping the bat and walking to the son of a bitch who is squirming against the wall, but knows it's useless.

"Why are you helping?"

"Because he touched Ana. For that alone, he's not allowed to breathe anymore."

Allen is silent for a minute, and then I see half a smile on his face. "Yeah, I'm going to help. You first, though, because I want to finish him."

I can't argue; given Allen's history, I'd demand that too.

"Batter up, then," I tell him, right before my bat drums into the side of our prey's head. I have to remind myself to pull my swings so Allen has something left to play with.

48
Ana

"You're home late. I thought we had to be at the dinner by now?" I ask Roman when he walks through the door. He stops to look at me and it takes years of training to keep from squirming. I know he's taking in my outfit and hair. I'm wearing dress pants, black, with a white lace and silk top. It shows nothing, not even cleavage. My hair, I've twisted and secured at my nape, and though I know I look good, I look nothing like Roman instructed. I wait to see if he says anything. I'm almost disappointed when he doesn't. "We're going to be late," I add, waiting for the explosion.

"I'll shower and be out in twenty," he says, which is damn anticlimactic. I've been keyed up for an hour wondering what he would say or do. I almost talked myself out of my rebellion two or three times. Now it seems I worried over nothing. I follow him to the bedroom and pick up his discarded trail of clothes.

I notice there's a stain on his shirt just as he heads to the shower. "Roman? Did you cut yourself? There's blood on your shirt."

"It's not mine," he says ominously over the roaring water in the shower. I decide to let it go and not think about it. Lord knows I have enough on my plate.

True to his word, Roman is out of the shower and in the limousine headed to the dinner in thirty minutes. Yet the ride over is really quiet. He's said very little and I'm picking up a weird vibe from him. Even worse, he's not given me so much as a simple kiss on the cheek since he got back, and that's very different from the way he usually is with me.

"Is everything okay, Roman?" I ask when I can't stand the silence any longer. We've been at the party for an hour. I've been introduced, inspected, and dissected since we got here. The men have leered and the women have been trying to kill me with looks. I'm a nervous wreck and I just want out of here. The fact that Roman has kept a hand on me the entire time, either by putting his arm around me or keeping one at the small of my back, is the only reason I haven't run away. All this, however, and he's still barely said more than four complete sentences to me. He leads me over to the corner of the ballroom we're in. We're the only couple in here and I find I can breathe easy for the first time since we got in the damn vehicle to get here.

"What could be wrong, pet?"

"You're quiet," I tell him as he pulls us to the corner and leans against it as if he owns the place. Hell, maybe he does. "Roman, maybe we should go home. You don't seem to be in the mood to be here, and I…"

"Stand in front of me, Ana, with your back to the others," he orders, interrupting me.

"What?"

"You heard me. Do it, Ana."

"What are you doing?" I ask, when he roughly pulls me so I'm standing between his legs.

"That's easy, pet. I'm going to play with my favorite toy," he tells me, his hand going to undo the button on my slacks.

"Roman, we're in the middle of a business party. They'll see!"

"Not if you're careful. Now, if you draw attention to us… probably."

"We can't do this," I tell him, even as my breathing speeds up and I look forward to his touch.

"It is happening. I think you forgot who has control," he

whispers into my ear, and chills run down my body as my heart speeds up. I should hate him when he talks like that. I should hate that he treats me as if I am his property. It shouldn't excite me the way it does. My body shouldn't betray me and become aroused until the point of pain, needing what only Roman can give me.

"I didn't forget. You would never let me forget," I tell him, and even to my ears, I sound like a petulant child.

"Interesting, because I could have sworn I told you to wear a particular dress tonight, and yet here you are in *pants*."

"The dress was too revealing. It showed everything I had."

"That's the problem. It's mine to reveal. Mine to control and mine to reward. I wanted every man in here to envy what is mine. To look, knowing they could never touch. *I like it, Ana.* I like knowing the sad fucks are home jacking off by their on hand and hating it because I have what they really want. I'm the one sunk balls-deep inside of her, making her scream. You took that away from me, pet. Now you have to pay the consequences."

"Roman…" I gasp his name as his hand slides into my loosened pants and cups my pussy, squeezing it.

"So warm and hot. This is my pussy now, Ana. *Mine.* It craves what I can give it," he growls in my ear as his fingers dive inside of me without warning. Jesus. How many did he thrust inside of me? More than one. Three, maybe? I can't be sure. The one thing I do know is that he's right. My pussy is so wet that it made his fingers thrust inside my channel easily. With each glide, and the teasing of his thumb against my clit, my desire increases, making me crave his cock. He's right. My body is his to control and it does need him. I hate myself because he has that control over me. I hate him because it's only my body he wants, not *me*… not my *heart*.

"One thing I should tell you, pet."

"What?" I ask and it sounds more like a moan.

"I'm going to finger-fuck you, just like this, for ten more minutes. The only catch is, you can't come until I tell you."

"Roman, I…"

"If you come, that would be bad. You didn't want to wear the dress I chose? If you come without permission, I won't care that everyone in here will see you. I'll strip you naked, bend you over this chair and fuck you until you tell everyone who you belong to." His words make my body shake and my orgasm build. My eyes close and I can picture him doing exactly that. Exactly.

Oh, God.

49

Roman

Ana trembles in my arms. I was pissed at her for defying me, but I have to admit, I love when she shows fire. Fuck, I love teaching her lessons, and this one might be the most enjoyable yet. Three fingers sink into that tight pussy. She's so fucking tight that even though she's drenched, it's hard to stretch her enough to get them inside of her. The scent of her arousal blooms around us as my thumb makes tiny circles against her throbbing clit. I push into it, holding it. It pulsates against my thumb the same way her walls are massaging against my fingers. It'd take so little to set her off. It makes me think my little Ana is an exhibitionist at heart.

"My pet is so greedy for my fingers. Does it turn you on, knowing I'm fucking you with a hundred people watching us? They're all wondering exactly what I'm doing to you, Ana."

"Jesus, Roman," she whispers, her hands biting into my shoulders as she tries to brace herself to keep from falling.

"Maybe we should show them. Would you like that, pet? Do you want me to get on my knees and eat out your juicy little cunt while they're all standing back there? Every man in here wants to be able to do that right now. They want between your legs. They want to bury their head so deep into your pussy and eat out this little cunt until your juice runs down their face and they drown in it while you ride them."

"Oh, fuck. Roman… I need…"

"I know what you need. You need me to…"

"Come. Oh, God. Baby, I need to come," she whimpers, her voice hoarse and raw. Her nails are biting into my skin. I can feel the muscles of her legs clench as her pussy presses down on my hand, trying to suck it further in and ride the hell out of it. She's already thrusting in rhythm with my hand, forgetting she has an audience. I spin her around, pinning her up against the wall, my body shielding her. I slow down my strokes, now. Letting my fingers glide in and out of her soaked little cunt, but going slow and methodical. It's not easy. That fucking pussy of hers is so hungry it clings to my fingers, grinding down on me every time they push into her.

"Roman, please stop torturing me," she whimpers.

In response, I bite into the side of her neck, giving her a sting of pain. I can feel her pussy quivering against my hand as even more moisture floods onto my fingers. I know that in one more thrust, one more bite, she's mine. She'll come so hard, she'll scream my name, not caring who can hear her. I'm a bastard enough to want that and I'd give it to her.

One thing holds me back. *She disobeyed me.* With that in mind, I stop completely. I pull my hand out from her warm depths with regret. I step back so she can watch me as I suck her sweet juice from my fingers. Fuck. Nothing in the world tastes like my Ana.

"Roman?" Her voice is confused and full of need.

I button her pants, leaning in at her ear so that only she can hear me. Fuckers are already trying to get closer to us, to get in on the show. "You don't get to come, pet. Maybe after we get home and you suck my cock and beg, maybe then. But if you want to defy me when I ask you for something, then that means you still need to learn who is in charge of your body." I pull away at her gasp, my hand going to her back to steer her back toward the crowd. She walks a step or two but resists me after a minute.

"But, Roman..."

"And Ana, if you even think of going to the restroom and making that sweet little pussy come, you won't sit still for a fucking week. Are we clear?"

Her eyes go round, her hand coming up to rub nervously against her throat. She nods her head once, watching me the entire time.

We're clear.

50

With every mile that brings us closer to downtown Miami, my heart hurts. The ride has been quiet, each of us in our own thoughts. We came home from the party last night and I thought everything was great. Roman pushed me up against the wall and buried his face between my legs, making me come twice before making slow love to me on the floor in front of the fireplace. We've made love a lot of ways, but none have been as sweet and slow as last night's had been.

I came so close to telling him I loved him. What would his reaction have been? The unknown of how he would react when he found out all my secrets was the only thing that held me back.

I was on the verge of my confession when we got the call. Someone had killed Big Joe. His body was thrown out in front of Roman's expensive club. His men called him the moment the body was discovered. I'm still in shock. I loved Big Joe. He was a mountain of a man with a soft side that he showed the women he protected. Roman held me while I cried, but since the call, I've seen the change in him. He's a man bent on revenge now. Completely business and cold in his demeanor. I understand it, even though I wish he could come back to me and be the man who made me feel alive last night.

"Did Joe have family?" I wonder aloud, not really asking Roman. I suppose I'm not even fully aware that I asked the question out loud. I just keep thinking what a shame it is that this world is robbed of such a good person.

"No one."

"That's sad. No one behind to mourn your passing," I

whisper. Roman doesn't respond. I didn't really expect him to. "Where are we going?"

"I'm going to drop you off at the apartment and then I have to go to the morgue to identify the body."

"I could go with you, Roman," I tell him, not wanting him to be without me—in the city, especially, as I'm more aware that Paul could try to set Roman up at any moment.

"No, Ana. I don't want you around any of this. I'll get it handled and check on your brother and then meet you back at the apartment."

"Maybe I should see my brother?" I suggest, not completely sure I want to at this point.

"He's getting better, Ana, but I don't want him around you. Not yet."

"Roman, you can't protect me from the world," I complain as we pull into the parking garage of Roman's apartment complex.

"I can try," he says with a ghost of a smile.

His face looks so tired. My hand reaches up to brush away the wrinkles that are gathered around his eyes. "I love you, Roman." My heart pounds in my chest. I didn't mean to say the words. They slipped out and now they're just hanging between us. I can't call them back and I can't make them unheard.

"Ana," he says, and I can read the regret there. You don't have to be a detective or a beat cop to see the writing on the wall.

"Shh... I didn't tell you because I expected anything back. I just wanted you to know." I'm half lying. I didn't tell him on purpose, but still it would have been nice to hear something back. Instead, I get a Roman who looks uncomfortable, a Roman who is rubbing the tension out of the back of his neck—tension my big mouth probably put there. The car comes to a stop and I turn the handle quickly, intent on getting out. Roman's hand on my arm stops me.

"We'll talk tonight, pet. I'll be back as soon as I can."

"Okay." I plaster a fake smile on my face. He holds my neck again and brings my lips to him. He gives me a sweet kiss, brief, but his tongue slides into my mouth, slow and seductive. "Be safe," I tell him before sliding out. One of his security guys is already waiting for me at the door. I need to get my head out of my ass and start figuring out what on earth I'm doing here. The only thing that is clear is that I've gone too far with Roman to ever find my way back to being the Ana I was before I went undercover, which means I need to try and protect Roman and get out from under Paul completely. I need to concentrate on that plan right now. Honestly, if I concentrated on the fact that I just told Roman I loved him and he didn't even bother to hide the look of surprise and regret in his face, I'd fall to my knees and cry. I can't do that. This seems like the safest option.

I walk into the apartment as if I'm on autopilot, and maybe I am, because I can't even remember the ride up in the elevator. I go straight to the bedroom and pull out my cellphone.

The asshole barely answers before I interrupt him. "Paul. We need to talk. I've decided to do what you want."

"What if I said I don't need you now?" he asks, and the implications of that scare the hell out of me.

"What if I told you I could deliver more than just what you asked? We need to meet." I'm bluffing my ass off here, but I don't have a fucking choice.

"Coffee shop on the corner. There's a small room off from the bathrooms. It will be unlocked. You have fifteen minutes and you better not be wasting my time, Ana."

"I'll be there." I tell him, closing my eyes and reminding myself that I don't have a choice.

51

Roman

I know who is behind Joe's murder. It doesn't take a rocket scientist. My mind is trying to stay on course, but hearing Ana tell me she loves me... *Fuck*.

I know how women get. She expects me to say that shit back. That's impossible. I don't believe in fucking love. Never had it in my life and I've seen enough of human nature to know that fucking shit doesn't exist. Nothing overrules human nature. When things get right down to it, survival is what matters most to people. No amount of feelings can outweigh that. Anything that says that it does is just some bastardized publicity. That's it.

All that said, I will admit to a perverse thrill at Ana's words. If I can nurture that and keep her trapped by my side, that's all I need. I'll make sure she never wants for a motherfucking thing. Keep her happy enough that she never questions about what else is out there.

As she disappears into the elevator with a security detail, I pick up the phone. I need to switch gears to business. I will have to plan shit out with Ana later.

My first move is to call Marcum to let him know what's going on.

"Hello?" A woman answers the phone. It's surprising because, as much as Marcum fucks around with chicks, not a damn one of them would ever answer this number.

"I'm looking for Marcum. Who is this?"

"This is his daughter-in-law, Tess. Marcum was in an accident."

"An accident?" I ask, instantly alert.

"Yeah, it was touch-and-go for a little while, but he'll be okay."

"What happened?"

"Can I ask who's calling?" she asks, instead of answering.

"Tell your father-in-law that his old friend from the neighborhood called and I'll be in touch," I tell her, hanging up. Marcum will understand who it is and I sure as fuck don't need to leave my name unless my job is the reason the son of a bitch ended up in the shape he's in.

Looks like I am going to have to handle Banks through a different manner. Kuzma, maybe, though I hesitate to go that route. I'm not going into business with the son of a bitch now, and owing him anything might not be an ideal situation. I need to think on this shit because if what happened with Joe is what I think, then I'll be seeing Banks soon.

Very fucking soon.

52

Ana

"You've got five minutes, Ana. Make it good," Paul barks, dragging me into the small room where I was to meet him.

I'm calling on every technique I ever learned to still my nerves and get through this meeting. I'm trained in meeting with the enemy and becoming part of their crowd. I just never imagined that the enemy would be the so-called good guys. Looking at Paul now—his black hair peppered around the edges, his face a mixture of worry and hatred, bags under his eyes, his jawline sallow and bloated, his stomach being more of a beer belly than the fit detective from my childhood—I wonder how I missed the signs. *Dirty cop.* I've heard the talk about them as I went through the academy; it hurts that the first one I encounter would be a man I looked up to.

"I still have the coke."

"So?"

"I know you asked me to plant it, but I have something better... *something bigger.*"

"What the fuck are you talking about, Ana?"

"I know where he's holding Allen. I can get him to take me there next week. You can follow us and bust him for kidnapping, attempted murder, and..."

"Why next week? If you had done what I asked you to do the first time, this would have been done."

"Okay, Paul. I'm going to level with you. You were right. I was losing my focus. I was falling under Roman's spell. But then I saw my brother. He's keeping him caged like a damn animal. He said he was going to kill him unless I did whatever he asked.

That's the only reason I went to his house with him. That's the only reason I couldn't talk to you. He's had me monitored night and day. I had to sneak out to even make it here today. I didn't have a choice."

"So you want me to twiddle my thumbs for a week while you maneuver Anthes into your trap?"

"It could work, Paul, and it would be so much more substantial than planting the coke on him, like your original plan."

"You know, Ana, I have to wonder why you keep mentioning my original plan. Actually, I'm wondering why you agreed to meet me at all after ignoring me for so long."

"I told you…"

"That you did, but I'm finding I don't really believe you."

"Paul…" My heart is beating erratically. It only increases when Paul reaches out and grabs my shirt. A man steps out of a dark corner of the room and I back away. I haven't seen this guy before and the look on his face is enough to scare me. "What's going on here?" I ask, proud when I don't sound like a scared little girl. I can't give Paul that satisfaction.

Paul reaches out and grabs me roughly by the arm, holding me even while I fight him. I'm trying to remember my combat training, but the defensive course which I should know and be able to do by pure instinct has somehow left me. I kick out, intent on gaining control of this situation again. That's when Paul's friend grabs me, bending my arms behind my back.

"I am having trouble trusting you, Ana. I think I'm going to have to test you."

"Test me?" I ask, trying to no avail to get free of the man's hold. Paul pulls out a large hunting knife and my blood runs cold. I'm so stupid. Why didn't I come more prepared? *What on Earth was I thinking?*

"Yeah, Ana. I've been at this a long time. I see the signs," he says, moving the side of the blade against my neck.

"Paul, you don't have to do this," I tell him, wishing I could get away from the man holding me prisoner. I'm afraid to move too much. The knife travels lower. I can feel the point of the blade now and it's making a path down my neck. He pushes in slightly. I feel a sting and then warm liquid. The bastard drew blood. The sick sadistic smile on his face tells me he not only drew blood—*he is enjoying it.*

"Oh, but I'm afraid I do," he tells me, and then all at once, he hooks my shirt into the blade of his knife and begins cutting. The fabric of my shirt slices in half, exposing my bra. Paul doesn't stop his knife until he cuts the bra in the same fashion, exposing my breasts. His hand comes up to cup them and I fight against my hold to try and get away. "Well, look at that. I guess you don't have a wire," he sneers, his cold fingers moving over my nipple. I'm seconds away from vomiting.

"You didn't have to do that," I whisper, wrapping my hands around my breast when the guy behind me finally lets me go.

"I'm afraid I did. Cheer up, Ana. It's not like I'm the only guy to have touched those fucking tits."

"What turned you into this... man?" I ask him, forcing myself to use that word because I want to call him a pig—or much, much worse.

"Just make sure you have Roman where you need him. Where is this fucking place anyway?"

"Now I think I'll take a page out of your playbook. I'll tell you when it's time. I don't want to risk you doing it before I can be there and make sure my brother survives the fight."

Paul looks me over grudgingly. "Look at that. I might make a cop out of you yet. I want my coke back since you can't manage to plant the shit."

"It's in the old apartment," I tell him, then mention where he can find it.

I don't breathe until they leave. Then I sink to the floor and let the tears fall. When this is all over, if I manage to survive, I'm going to kill Paul. I don't for one second think it will make me feel better, but if ever a man deserved to die, it is him. How I went for so long without seeing the monster beneath amazes me. I've seen it now, however, and I will put a bullet into him without blinking.

It takes me another ten minutes before I can finally pull myself together. I look around the small room. There's a few t-shirts with the place's name emblazoned on them. I yank off my ruined clothes, throw them in the trash, then pull a t-shirt on, wondering if I'll get arrested for theft before I can get out of this fucking place. That would cap off a perfect day.

53
Roman

Something is going on with Ana. I'm not sure what it is, but for the last three days, she's withdrawn and seems to be somewhere else. The only time I feel she's even halfway with me is when we're fucking. I'll have to figure it out, but I can't right now. There's too much shit going down. *Like today.*

We're standing by the grave of one of the few men I considered a friend, listening to some preacher go on about finding a better life in another world. It sounds lame to my ears. The world is a cold, dark place, and having Joe gone just makes it more so. The only warmth in my life is the woman standing beside me right now, crying. I wrap my arm around her, pulling her into me. She buries her face in my chest and I kiss the top of her head, wishing I could take away her pain—fuck, wishing I could take my own. It's my fault Joe is being buried. He was killed to send me a message, a message I received loud and clear, and one I'm going to deliver twofold on that sorry fuck, Paul Banks.

I have a meeting with Kuzma tonight. I hesitated to go this route, but the old adage "go big or go home" seemed apt. I'm going to make Banks sorry he was ever born. Big Joe deserves that.

The graveside service ends. Ana and I each place a rose on top of the coffin and start walking back to the limo. Robert is standing by the vehicle waiting, and I have two of my best security detail walking behind me. I can't take a chance with Ana's safety. We're almost to the car when Banks and four others get out of a white sedan across from my limo. Ana goes rigid in my arms, and with good reason. I can tell Banks is up to no good, and dealing with him is the last fucking thing I want to do.

"Banks. What the fuck are you doing here?"

"Can't a man pay his respects?" he asks with a cocky look on his sullen face. I clench my hand into a fist and it takes all I have not to level him. The bastard is baiting me. I can see it, and I keep my face unreadable.

"A *man* probably could. Still doesn't explain why *you're* here," I tell him, the barb subtle but pretty fucking clear. I know he understands, it shows in his face.

"You think you're smart, don't you, Anthes? I think it might be time to bring you down a peg or two."

"You can try," I tell him, growing bored with the game. "Ana, go wait for me in the car," I tell her, motioning for one of the security members to follow her.

"Roman, I don't think that would be a good idea. Maybe..." Ana starts.

Before I can respond, Banks joins in. "Yeah, Roman, I don't think that'd be a good idea either."

Banks thrusts a piece of paper at me. I grab it, moving in front of Ana to protect her from the man. It's an instinctual move; he'll never get close enough to hurt her.

"What is this?"

"A warrant. We got a tip you're carrying drugs in your car."

"That's ridiculous, Banks," I tell him, shaking my head and pinching the bridge of my nose in frustration. I need to call my attorney to handle this. I don't have time for this shit.

"Maybe, but we're going to need to check your limo out, just in case. Just doing our job, you understand," he says with a self-satisfied grin on his face.

The men behind him are already moving to the car.

Something about the whole situation stinks, and I'm not just talking about the way Banks looks entirely too confident. Instantly, that gut instinct I have comes alive. I look at Bruno behind me. I don't have to give him the words; he knows what I want. He nods and I know he'll have a call through to my attorney in seconds if this all goes south, which I'm pretty sure it will. As if on cue, one of the men with Banks speaks up.

"Detective, we found something," they shout.

My eyes go in that direction as the man in question pulls out a couple kilos of wrapped and tightly-packed blow, as well as two guns. There's also a closed briefcase. I've never seen the shit before, but that doesn't surprise me in the least.

"Roman," Ana cries, her nails biting into my arm.

"Ana, my attorney will have this sorted out in no time. You go with Bruno and…"

"That won't be necessary. Ana is going nowhere," Paul says, his face telling me he think he has completely control. He better savor this victory; it will be his last, and it will be nowhere near as monumental as he thinks.

"You have no control over me. That's my car, and Ana has nothing to do with this," I growl, more irritated than anything. I don't want this shit touching Ana.

"That's where you're wrong, Anthes. Ana here is key in all of it."

Something in the way Paul says her name and the wait Ana pulls away from me, stiffening, alerts me to a shift in the game. I look down as Ana steps away. There's tears in her eyes, and she's ringing her hands.

"Roman, you need to understand…"

"What Ana here is trying to say…" Paul interrupts her, coming to stand by her and pull her into his side. I lash out without hearing the rest of his sentence, intent only on tearing her away from him, all of my calm leaving me—but then again, ever since Ana came into my life, I've never been myself.

Two of Paul's henchmen grab me. I throw them off easily, thinking of only saving Ana. That's when the Taser gun hits me and I drop to my knees, my body shaking. I fight against its pull, looking up at Banks and plotting his death as electricity runs through my body. Banks throws something on the ground that lands in front of my knees. His men are clicking the handcuffs behind my back, securing me. My eyes are blurry and I try to shake off the effects to focus.

I see Ana's picture and a badge.

Officer Ana Stevens.

I look back at her and tears are running down her face. She's wrenched herself away from Banks, but now that is of little comfort. Undercover cop, and probably one of the ones that set this little dog and pony show up. Something inside of me twists and breaks, and I concentrate on the pain. Banks pulls me up and I let him. After the Taser, I can't seem to fucking get control enough to stop him. *Officer Ana Stevens. Fucking traitorous bitch.* It would almost be humorous that I've been taken in by the woman I had at first planned to use. Funny as hell, if it didn't hurt.

As he pushes me into the back of a squad car, my eyes catch Ana's one last time. She's saying something I can't hear her through the window, and I don't want to. I turn away from her.

I'm done.

54
Ana

Shell-shocked. That's the only way to describe the last month. I had watched as they hauled Roman away. The smug look of satisfaction on Paul's face as he sneered at me was almost as bad as the betrayal shining in Roman's.

I love him and he hates me. He has good reason. In all the scenarios where I told Roman who I really was, I never once thought I wouldn't get the chance to try and explain. Roman won't see me though. I've been trying, and each time he ignores me.

Instead, I've spent my time cleaning out my locker at the station and ignoring the snarls and looks of my once fellow cops, wadding up the sticky notices that littered my locker declaring me a snitch and sometimes much worse. I go through meeting after meeting with IAB, turning in every bit of evidence I had gathered against Paul Banks and the three men that worked under him and doing my best to make Roman appear to be a poster child for clean living magazine.

It worked. Roman's charges were dismissed. I was stripped of my badge and reprimanded, but any charges that might have been filed against me were negated in exchange for helping with IAB's investigation. I might have not been wearing a wire each time I met with Paul, but I had been using a mini voice recorder in my pocket, catching Paul's instructions and plans each time. The best evidence came, however, when I informed the detective in charge about a small firebox that Paul kept in his home office. It was a gamble. I remembered it from the times during my training that I would join Paul and several other squad members for a cookout and we planned the best way to set me up to meet Roman. I didn't realize what a complete moron Paul was until IAB found the trophies Paul kept from every crooked deal he ever made. He was using the proof inside to blackmail members of the squad to do his bidding, but in the end, the proof only helped to arrest him. If karma is real at all, it should lock him up for a long fucking time. His trial is scheduled to begin soon, and I for one can't wait.

That's not what tonight is about, however. Tonight is a last ditch effort. I'm at the strip club. I know Roman won't be here, but he'll be told I am, especially when I demand to dance. I was never fired, so technically I'm still on staff. It will probably blow up in my face, but maybe Roman will at least come here to talk to me.

Okay, as plans go, it's shit. I know it. I just know I have to try. *I have to.* I kept expecting him to reach out to me, especially when he found out that I had cleared his name at the expense of my career. *I heard nothing.* I thought he would at least talk to me when I showed up at the Stable demanding to see him after Paul was arrested.

I was escorted off the premises. Which leads me to now. I don't have any hope held out that tonight will end differently than the other numerous times I've tried. However, it is my last time to try. If I don't see Roman tonight, I walk away. It won't be what I want, but I need to move forward with my life. Besides, I'm getting pissed at him. I know he's mad and he gets to be angry, but to just refuse to talk to me and walk away as if we were nothing to each other...?

"Ana? What the fuck are you doing here?"

I stop in front of the back dressing rooms, shock flooding through my system. Of all the people I thought would be here tonight, this wasn't one of them.

"Allen? What—I mean, *how...* When did this happen? "

"I'm working for Roman a few nights a week. Just to see..."

"See what? Why would he let you work for him? I don't understand," I mumble, thoroughly confused. What am I missing here? And why does Allen seem... almost normal? What happened to the angry brother who hated the world? I have so many questions, but before I can ask them, Allen is grabbing my hand.

"You need to get out of here," he grumbles, his grip firm as he tries to pull me away. I jerk against his hold, easily breaking free.

"I'm not going anywhere. Tonight is my regular night to dance," I announce. Allen's eyes go wide and he shakes his head in disbelief. I try to stand tall at my announcement, but avoid looking into Allen's eyes. The last thing I need is for him to read the panic in them.

"Are you crazy?" Allen cries. "Roman isn't going to let you dance!"

"Well, he didn't fire me. Until he does, I'm dancing."

"Ana, you're being stupid. If Roman finds out you're here, he'll have you escorted out of the club so fast your head will spin. Hell, as mad as he is at you right now, he may have you arrested for trespassing."

"Then he'll have to be the one to tell me that himself, won't he? And when did you become Roman's right hand man, anyway?"

"I'm trying to change, and Roman's helping. I'd be glad to talk to you about it. Some other time. Not tonight. There's shit going on and I need you out of this club."

"There's always shit going on. Allen, I can't leave. I have to talk to Roman," I finally tell him, desperation and honesty breaking through my stupid plan.

"Ana, he doesn't want to talk to you right now. You need to give him time. He…"

"He has had time! I at least deserve him telling me that he hates me and never wants to see me again! He owes me that!"

"I don't owe you anything, Ana."

I freeze when Roman's voice interrupts. I turn around slowly to look at the man who has haunted my dreams. He looks as good as he ever did, his suit impeccable, his hair a little longer, but I like it. He has circles under his eyes and a five o'clock shadow that I've never seen on him before. It looks good.

"We need to talk, Roman," I tell him and hope like hell my courage doesn't disappear.

55

Roman

I hate her. At least that's what I've been trying to tell myself. People don't lie to me and live. They sure as fuck don't betray me as deeply as Ana did. I've cut her out of my life. I'm done. Those are all things that I've repeated to myself over and over the last month. Things that I tried to drum into my head even as I would jack off to the memory of her sweet pussy draining me dry. I thought I had succeeded. I was able to function through the day now instead of wanting to drown myself in booze. The only time I allowed my obsession with her to overtake me was when I was home alone. That had to be progress.

One look at her tonight, and I know I've been lying to myself. She's wearing faded jeans, the fabric worn so much the once dark blue color is practically the color of ice, faded and cold. My fingers itch to hold her ass and see just how soft the cloth would feel. She has on a black t-shirt and it makes her look pale and washed out, but even with that, she's the most beautiful woman I've ever seen in my life.

"We have nothing to say to each other, Ana. You can leave peacefully or I'll have Bruno escort you."

"Boss, I can take her home. Ana and I need to talk anyway," Allen interjects.

Over the past month, Allen has made great strides. I'm even starting to like the kid. I, however, don't want his interference here.

"You need to go back to work, Allen," I tell him, not taking my eyes off Ana.

"Ana," Allen says, and she puts her hand in his and squeezes it. He's her goddamn brother and that small touch fires jealousy inside of me. I need to get her the fuck out of here before I crumble.

Allen leaves. I never take my eyes away from Ana, and she's staring right back at me. I can pick up her nervousness, but then again, I've always been attuned to Ana and her body. *Her body.* Jesus, she looks good. Her curves seems fuller, her lips more prominent. What harm would come from just one small sip from them?

"You need to leave," I order again, my voice gruffer as I fight the hard-on that's pressing against the zipper of my slacks.

"I don't want to. I don't think you want me to either, Roman," she says, taking a step towards me. It's all I can do not to back away from her.

"You would be wrong. For some strange reason, I don't keep women around who think they can play me."

"I was doing my job," she says, her face flushed.

"You betrayed me. I don't give people a second chance to do that, Ana."

"I need you to give me one," she says, and her hand reaches out and touches my stomach. I want to groan when electricity charges between us, firing through my blood and making my dick jerk in reaction. People around us have grown quiet. It's then I remember we're standing at the dressing rooms of the other girls. I grab her hand on my stomach and practically pull her down the small hall. I don't stop until we make it into the back room where the private dances are held. This is where the minx tortured me in the beginning; it seems apt that this is where it should end. It's deserted when we get there, though I know it will be busy in here soon. I lock the door and turn back to Ana. Her breathing is so ragged, it shakes her body, her face even more flushed. Those violet eyes are dilated. I try to swallow down my need.

"Ana, you need to go."

"I came here to dance," she says, kicking off her shoes. I watch her and I'm at war with myself, knowing I need to send her away, but wanting one last taste of her. And why shouldn't I? She owes me. I'm still who I am. I can take this and send her away. She wants to play the whore? Why shouldn't I let her? Surely that's the only reason I don't stop her when she peels those jeans down over her hips, revealing the peach-colored flesh I want to bite into. They slide further down her legs and she gracefully kicks them off.

Fuck it. Let her dance. I sit in a cushioned chair, waiting and hoping like hell I manage to look bored because I'm anything but.

"I've missed you Roman," she whispers, lifting her shirt over her head.

"If you want to dance, Ana, then dance. But I don't need the commentary," I warn her, my voice cold.

I can't hear her say words that shouldn't mean a damn thing to me. It shouldn't matter in the least that she misses me. I don't miss the fire in her eyes at my words. I'm pissing her off. Good. She should be pissed off. She should feel anger, because it's all that I've felt since that day in the cemetery. Nothing has made it better. Even learning that she told the court that she planted all of the shit on me under orders of a superior officer did nothing to soothe my anger. I wanted to choke her. I wanted to scream and kill her. *I wanted to fuck her.* No matter the anger and hate inside of me, it always boiled down to that. I wanted to sink into her tight little cunt and fuck her so hard and raw that she'd never walk right again.

I still want that. As she stands in front of me in her silk underthings now, I want it so much my damn cock is salivating in need. Until Ana, I was all about control. Now I have none. *Not a fucking drop of it.*

She walks towards me, her hips swaying in tune to some imaginary music. *Black silk.* She's wearing black silk underwear and it never looked so fucking good. She bypasses the pole and I mourn it. I'd love to see her grinding up against it, spinning around, opening her legs…

All thoughts of it stop, however, when she stands in front of me. She puts her hands on my shoulders and leans down so her breasts are in front of my face. It might be my imagination, but they look larger than I remember, so fucking ripe and big that I could push my cock into their depths and wrap them tight around my shaft and fuck myself with them. I resist… *barely.*

Her finger nails drag down my chest, stopping at my tie, and she quickly undoes it with just a few easy moves. I'd be impressed if my eyes weren't glued to the way her hips are moving as if she's sliding back and forth on my cock. She leans down and, as she unbuttons my shirt, her tongue licks a path down my chest. My hands bite into the armrest of the chair I'm in to keep from touching her. It's a wonder I don't break off the damn thing.

"I thought you didn't do private dances," I grumble, my voice hoarse.

Ana stops and looks at me, her eyes full of desire. Against my will, my hand goes to my cock, which is rock hard, and I grab it, squeezing it tight to try and hold the fucker back from coming in my damn pants. *Not again.* Not…

All thought stops when Ana unhooks her bra and throws it to the floor. Next, she slides down the barely-there scrap of lace that had covered her pussy. The lips of that juicy cunt are plump and covered in her desire, slick and wet to the eye, and I breathe in the scent of her arousal. What man could resist that?

Especially when they know firsthand how fucking good it is.

"I'll let you in on a secret, Roman," she says, sinking to her knees between my legs. I don't stop her when she starts undoing my belt. If anything, I widen my legs. She wants fucked? I can fuck her. Doesn't mean I won't send her on her way when it's done.

"What's that?" I ask, closing my eyes as she lowers the zipper and snakes her hand inside to wrap it around my dick.

"I didn't come here to dance for you," she whispers before sliding my cock in her mouth and devouring it.

Against my will, my hand tangles in her hair as I watch inch by inch of my shaft disappear in that sweet haven. She doesn't stop, sliding down on my dick and letting it stretch her mouth. She takes me all the way to the back of her throat, only stopping when her nose is pushed up against the small nest of curls on my body. I feel the small puffs of air hit my skin as she breathes. She starts to pull off my dick, and I selfishly tighten my hold on her hair, not letting her, needing to savor this moment. Finally, I'm the one who pulls her off of my dick. My fingers so tangled in her hair, I know it's hurting her, but she doesn't fight. I drag her face up to mine, admiring the way her lips shine with a combination of her saliva and my pre-cum. They're puffy from the rough way I moved her head on my dick. *Beautiful.*

"You want fucked, Ana? I'll fuck you. It's not going to change anything," I warn her, or maybe myself. "You need a dick, I'll give it to you." I growl again before taking her mouth with my own.

56

Ana

I take Roman's kiss, and it's a punishing kiss. It's a kiss full of anger, betrayal, and *desire*. I take it, even as his words wound me. His tongue pushes into my mouth, hard and unforgiving. I let him conquer my mouth, drinking in his taste. If all I get is this one night, then I'm going to take it and hopefully live on it the rest of my life.

When we break apart, we're both breathing hard. He holds me prisoner by the way he has my hair. He roughly turns me so my back is to him, lifting me up on his lap so I'm forced to straddle his legs. His grip on my hair lets go, but only to be replaced by an equally punishing grip on my hip as he holds me suspended in the air.

"Is this what you want, Ana? Did you come here like a dog in heat needing my cock?" he growls, his words wounding me while at the same time sending my desire up another notch. There's nothing I can say to him that will reach him. I understand that now. So be it. If this is the end of whatever we were to each other, there's nothing I can do. So I give him the only words he wants from me.

"Fuck me, Roman," I tell him.

He doesn't answer, not with words. He growls out at me. His voice raw and untamed like a wounded animal and I can hear what he thinks I don't. I hear the hurt and anger mixed in it. It's not my imagination; it permeates the air around us. *I did that. I betrayed Roman.* I swallow down the wave of sadness inside of me and concentrate on the here and now. He thrusts me down on his cock, slamming into me with so much force that it feels like he might tear me apart. Fear hits me for a moment. I want him, but I can't let him... I grab his hand from my hip and pull it up my side and to my breast. I knead my breast with it while rotating my hips and grinding my pussy against his dick. Soon, his other hand joins in and he's holding both of my breasts while I ride him. I'm tightening the muscles of my pussy against his shaft, moving up and down on him and riding him in a way I know will bring him the most pleasure—in the way he taught me to ride him.

"You feel so good, Roman. I love the way you fill me, so big and wide I can taste you when you're inside of me."

"Shut up, Ana," he growls, his hands punishing my breasts in a way I know will leave bruises.

"I need you, Roman. I've been so lost without you," I tell him, my head going back against his shoulder as my body rides him faster, twisting my hips to the side so he rakes against the soft walls of my pussy. He's so warm and hot, filling me so tightly that I swear I can feel the ridges of his dick inside me, scraping every nerve ending I have.

"You just needed fucking. Any dick would do, Ana. It's just sex."

"I'll never have anyone but you inside of me, Roman," I answer him honestly. "Oh, God, baby. I'm going to come."

"Goddamn you, Ana," he groans, but I can feel the way his muscles tighten. He's getting ready to come too.

"Please, Roman, give me your cum. Unload it all in me. Give me enough to keep me warm even after you send me away," I cry beyond the point where I can feel shame. Giving him honesty is so much easier when I don't have to see him and can just let go and stare straight ahead, losing myself in the sensations he's drawing from my body.

"Fuck," he moans from behind me, his hands leaving my

breasts to slide down my sides to my hips. One goes even further, not stopping until his fingers find my clit. He manipulates it and I cry out his name on a low, whining moan as my climax thunders through my body. I can feel myself coming all over his shaft as spasm after spasm shakes me to my core. My hands are biting into the arms of the chair as I lose myself. I hear Roman's roar a moment later and then feel the first hot splash of cum inside of me, followed by another and another. I continue riding him through his own orgasm, unable to do anything but feel.

"I love you, Roman. I love you," I whisper. "I'll always love you."

57

Roman

She's destroyed me. I thought she had before, but I had no idea. As I'm left sitting here with Ana resting against my chest and the final aftershocks of my orgasm finishing, I know now. She's destroyed me. The cries of her telling me she loved me are still echoing in my ears. What the fuck am I supposed to do with that? I give myself a couple moments before I pull her off of me. I can't breathe. I need to distance myself from this. *From her.* She stands, almost falling. I stand up, zipping up my pants and needing to get away. Needing to get away from her body... Fuck, I'm choking on the scent of her.

"Roman?"

I can't look back at her. I can't. "I can't do this, Ana. I'm not giving you an opportunity to betray me again. I'm not a man who does love. That doesn't exist. The only instinct that matters is survival," I tell her when I reach the door, my back to her.

"Let me in, Roman. I promise you I'll make sure you never regret it. Please, don't shut me out."

My hand trembles with the need to give in. She'll never know how much I want to do exactly that.

"Goodbye, Ana."

"Goodbye, Roman," she says, her voice hoarse with tears. I hear them and I feel like a bastard for being the cause of them. I am a bastard. I'm pushing her out of my life. When I found out about her betrayal, something inside of me broke. I've always managed to be detached in life. Ana stopped that. Her betrayal nearly brought me to my knees and that is unacceptable. No one will have that control over me again. No matter how much I may wish it was different.

I walk out of the room and keep going. Allen stops me at the door, I know he's worried about his sister, but I can't talk to him. Right now, I don't think I can talk to anyone. If I did, the only words I'd want to say would be begging Ana not to leave.

"Take your sister home, Allen. Make sure she doesn't come back," I growl, opening the door. When the night air hits me, it does nothing to drive away Ana's scent. I have a feeling nothing ever will.

It's over.

Three Months Later

"What are you two doing? I can't believe you kidnapped me! Do you know there are laws against this?" I cry, my heart still racing in my chest.

I'm in the back of Roman's limousine with Bruno. Allen is driving. Apparently, the mole on the inside of Roman's business was Robert, and he used the maid Mayra as his personal spy. No wonder the bitch had it out for me from the start. Allen told me that a month ago. It surprised me, but I was glad that Roman finally knew who the guy in his organization was. I was relieved even though it had nothing to do with me anymore—which is why I'm panicked at the thought of being in Roman's car.

I made a clean break from Roman. I even moved to Georgia to start my life over again. The last thing I need is to be anywhere near him right now. My hand goes to my stomach—my *very* pregnant stomach. There's definitely no hiding the baby bump now. No, at almost six months pregnant, there's no hiding. I pull the heavy coat I'm wearing tighter around me. At least Allen gave me this coat. I don't know what he's doing, but I need something to hide the fact that I'm pregnant from Roman if I see him again.

"The boss needs you," Bruno says, or rather, *repeats*. That's all he or Allen have been saying since they broke into my house before dawn this morning and manhandled me into the limo. Okay, *carried*—and rather delicately, really, considering I'm getting so fat.

"And I told you, I doubt Roman would want me anywhere

near him. Whatever is going on, you need to find someone else to help him," I respond, not bothering to ask what in the world he needed me for, since they haven't answered the other hundred times I've asked.

Silence.

I didn't expect anything else. It's evening now and, except for a few quick stops for restroom and food breaks, we've driven all day. In fact, I figure in an hour I'll be at Roman's house. With each mile that we travel, my nerves and panic kick up. When we turn into Roman's private driveway, I can literally taste my fear.

"Allen, please don't do this. Take me back home."

"Sis, Roman—"

"I don't want him to keep me because he knows I'm pregnant, Allen. I deserve better than that," I tell him, and then it hits me. "Oh, God. Is that it, Allen? Does Roman know I'm pregnant and wants to take my baby?" My hand goes to my stomach, wrapping around it as if to protect him from the unknown threat.

Allen stops the car to look back at me. He cups my shoulder gently with understanding. If anything good has come out of this whole mess, it's that Allen and I have grown close.

"He doesn't know about the baby, Ana. I promise you. You are needed. You'll understand when you see him." I swallow, unable to hide the panic on my face. "I promise that I will take you back home the moment you ask me, Ana. Trust me."

I bite my lips, but shake my head yes. There's little I can do about it now.

"I'll be outside for an hour, Ana. Just come out if you need me," Allen says a little later when he opens the front door.

"You're leaving me?" I ask, nearly choking on the fear.

"I'll just be outside, sis. I promise."

I close my eyes as the shutting of the door sounds so final.

My nose wrinkles at the musty smell of Roman's house. It always smelled like fresh outdoors and pine. Did his cleaning crew quit? I walk through the darkened foyer, my hand automatically feeling for the light switch on the wall because the house is completely dark. Fear swamps me. I pull the coat more towards my front, doing my best to hide my baby-bump. Was Roman in an accident? Did something happen? Is that why they wanted me here?

"Roman?" I call out, my voice little more than a whisper. When I hear nothing back, I take a breath and try to strengthen myself. "Roman?"

I stop and listen. I hear the faint sound of someone coming from Roman's den. I make my way there, turning on the lights. What I see in the main living room stops me in my tracks. There are empty liquor bottles everywhere, Styrofoam containers that, from the smell, now contain remnants of moldy take-out. I pull one back just to be sure and instantly close it when I take in the green and white remnants of what I think used to be a half-eaten hamburger. There's empty soda cans and pizza boxes too. The once pristine white carpet will probably never be clean again. *What the hell has been going on here?*

I make it to the den, my hand stalling on the doorknob as I gather up what little courage I have. I open it, my nose curling in disgust. The stench is even worse in here. The room is completely dark. I flip on a lamp that's on a table by the door. The room floods with light and it takes a minute for my eyes to adjust. Even then, it takes me a minute to understand what I'm seeing. Roman is laying on the floor, his hair grown out ridiculously long for him, the dark bangs lying haphazardly over his eyes. He's wearing a t-shirt that I think is supposed to be white, but has obviously been through a war with beer and pizza—and lost. He has on gray jogging pants that are riding low on his hips and he's staring straight at me, his eyes bloodshot.

"Roman?" I ask, because God's honest truth, I can't be sure. The man I'm staring at is nothing like the Roman, I know.

"The bitch who haunts me," he slurs. "What are you doing here, pet? You're early. You're not supposed to haunt my dreams until I pass out." He holds up a half empty bottle of whiskey, shaking it at me. "I still have some to go before I get there."

Dear Lord. "Roman, what happened to you?"

"As if you didn't know. You poisoned me," he growls, and I have no idea what he is talking about.

"Roman," I start, but he interrupts me.

"I can't eat, I can't sleep, I can't even fucking breathe without you in my head, your taste on my tongue, your fucking scent filling my lungs. I told you to leave, Ana. I told you to get the fuck away from me. Why won't you leave me alone to die in peace?" he growls at me, except it's not at me. I get the feeling he doesn't think I'm really here.

I rub my palm across my forehead. Of all the things I expected, this wasn't it. There's no talking to Roman like this. I don't even know what this means. The only thing that is clear is that he's missed me. He's been as miserable as I have. If I hadn't had the baby to think about these months without him, would I have been in much the same shape? Probably.

Roman might not realize it, but we're made for each other. I pick up the phone and dial Allen's cell.

"Sis?"

"You and Bruno need to come help me sober up the father of my child."

"Sis?" he asks again.

"You got me here, Allen. Now help me," I order him, hanging up. I look over at Roman who is snoring now, and I can almost smile.

As soon as my head quits trying to kill me, I'm going to fire Bruno and Allen. I wince as the light from the window shines through, the blinds pulled up. Who the fuck did that? And why am I in this damn room? I don't sleep in this bed. I can't sleep in this bed. Ana haunts me here.

Fuck. She haunts me everywhere.

I look down at the bed and notice there are clean sheets on it. Even so, I can still smell the faint trace of Ana's perfume on them. My dick jerks awake, but I ignore the fucker. He and I both are getting tired of using my hand. I get out of bed, frowning when I see a clean pair of jogging pants lying across the nightstand. I slip them on, ignoring how even the slightest movement causes pain to radiate through my joints and center in the mother of all hangovers that has taken up residence behind my eyes. Even my fucking teeth hurt. I'm way too fucking sober. I've been drunk for months now and today is not the day to try being sober. I walk out of the room, intent on finding another bottle of whiskey and maybe some leftover pizza. I think there's some left in one of the boxes in the kitchen.

I stop when I enter the den and there are three women in uniforms cleaning the room. They're wearing black pants and gray shirts that proclaim them "Helping Hand Maid Service". *What the fuck?* I wrench a vacuum cleaner out of the hand of one of them and shut the son of a bitch off.

"Who the hell are you and what are you doing in my house?" I growl, the roar of my voice hurting me, but not nearly as much as the vacuum was doing. The ladies look at me like I'm the insane one, which is crazy because they're the ones trespassing. "I mean it! I want to know what the fuck you are doing here and who let you in!"

"They're cleaning."

My breath lodges in my chest and I'm afraid to fucking turn around—afraid it's her, afraid it's not. Jesus.

"Ladies, if you could, go ahead and move to the kitchen. We can finish in here after Mr. Anthes and I talk."

They hustle out, and still I'm unable to turn around. I take the coward's way out and, instead, walk to the window. I stare out at the rolling green grass of my yard and try to figure out exactly what is going on.

"What are you doing here, Ana?" I ask when I can't stand the silence any longer.

"Bruno and Allen came and got me. They said you needed me."

"I didn't ask them to," I grumble, my hand coming up to rub my chin.

"I know. Were they telling me the truth?"

"About what?"

"Do you need me, Roman?"

Yes, my brain screams out, but I don't say that. I can't. I go to turn around instead, needing to figure out how to talk to her and make her stay without giving in. "Ana..."

"Don't turn around, Roman. If you're just going to send me away again, keep your back turned to me. You owe me that. I don't want to have to see your face if all you are going to do is send me away again. I can't handle that."

"Have you missed me, Ana?"

"With every breath that I draw," she whispers, and it feels like there's this fist around my heart. Her confession is raw and maybe I just want to believe it. I'm not sure, but it feels honest. It feels like truth, so I give her one of my own.

"I miss you too, pet."

"Then don't send me away again, Roman. Let me come home. I know my lies hurt you, but I never lied about anything that was important. I love you."

Let her come home. Does she have any idea how much I want that? Does she know what it did to me to know that I pushed her away thinking she had planted evidence on me, only to find out Robert had done it? Does she have any idea the hell I've gone through knowing I pushed away my only chance at happiness? I used to think love was a lie invented by Hollywood, a dream created to sell books and movies. Survival was the only thing I understand, and maybe it still is, because I know I need Ana in my life to survive. Without her, I don't want to. I don't want to live one more day without her.

"Ana? Can I turn around now, if I ask you to stay?" I question, my voice thick. I look down at my hands and they're shaking.

"Are you going to ask me to stay?" she asks, her voice breaking.

"No," I tell her, turning. My eyes instantly lock onto her. "I'm going to beg..." My voice trails off because I'm standing there drinking in the woman I adore. I drink her in, her sun-kissed blonde hair shining, her violet eyes full of tears. The lavender sundress she's wearing joins in and it all comes together to make her more beautiful than even I remembered.

The thing that freezes my voice and makes any further words impossible though is the obvious swell of her stomach.

Ana. My Ana, is... *pregnant.*

I see the exact moment Roman discovers I'm pregnant. I'm okay with it. After spending the night in his arms, him holding me even as he was sleeping, him whispering my name when I curled into him, I knew. He might not have said it and maybe he never will, but Roman loves me. That was evident in the way he came unraveled without me, in the way he held me last night. He loves me. I can live without the words because I feel them.

Still, even knowing that, this morning I was nervous. I was prepared to fight Roman tooth and nail to get him to admit that he needed me. Knowing he's caving easily makes it all okay.

"Ana?" he asks, a look of disbelief on his face and maybe, just maybe happiness. My hand goes to my stomach, rubbing it softly.

"Surprise?" I half tell, half ask.

"You're pregnant?"

"Yeah," I tell him, panicking. Is he going to get mad about this? Because I didn't tell him? Will he see that there was no way I was going to force him to accept me in his life, if he didn't want me?

"We're having a baby?"

I bite my lip and try to remember to breathe.

"A little boy."

"You already know?" he asks, his eyes moving from my stomach to my eyes as he walks to me.

"Yeah." I'm unsure of what else to say.

"We're having a baby," he whispers, dropping to his knees in front of me, his large hand caressing each side of my stomach as he places a kiss in the middle of it. Little Roman apparently didn't like that because he kicks out against his dad's kiss.

Roman's head snaps back and he looks up at me and I can't help but smile.

"I think he might be a football player," I tell him, placing my hand over one of Roman's and bringing it back to the spot on my stomach where the baby likes to push. In just a minute or two, I feel the fluttering sensation as the baby delivers a well-timed kick.

"Oh my God. That's our baby," Roman says, at a loss for words and acting in ways I never thought I'd see him.

"It is," I tell him, my fingers tangling in his hair.

"We're going to have a baby," he says again, but I see the happiness in his face and something shifts inside of me.

"We are. We're going to be a family, Roman."

"You're never leaving me, Ana. I can't make it without you," he says, allowing the fear to cloud his eyes briefly before that bone-melting dominant look returns, and his hand wraps in my hair. He brings our lips together for a kiss and right before his claims mine, he murmurs against them. "You're never getting away from me again, pet." I let his claim echo through my body, healing the empty spots inside of me that are remaining, and take his kiss. I don't answer, because there's nothing else to say.

I never want to leave Roman. I'm home to stay.

EPILOGUE
TAKE TWO

Ana

Roman Allen Anthes was born on November 14th at three in the morning after making me go through forty-two hours of grueling labor and nearly causing his father to go insane. It was all worth it though, and when I look at the child who is turning six months old today, I couldn't imagine life being more complete.

"Is mommy's baby, hungry?" I ask him, reaching down into the crib. He instantly stops crying and he reaches out to me with his little hands, knowing what comes next.

I take him to the rocking chair that Roman surprised me with when we were fixing up the nursery. It's a beautiful handmade piece that I will cherish the rest of my life. I pull the strap from my dress and adjust my breast so the baby can begin to nurse. He latches on and greedily drinks up. It took some getting used to, but I love breastfeeding. It sounds hokey, but it feels as if by doing it, I'm affirming nature's grand design. I even feel beautiful, even if my body is never going to get back to the shape it was in before Roman Jr. decided to wreck it.

I begin rocking slowly. Not enough movement to jar him, but just a soft, rhythmic movement that he likes. I hum his favorite lullaby. Pretty soon, his hungry grunts and swallows fill the room as his little hand wraps around my finger. I kiss his forehead and commit this to memory. Another beautiful memory in a lifetime of them. That's what life with Roman has given me. I'm the luckiest woman on the face of the Earth. I feel that in my soul. Roman and I might have started off rocky, but the ride was more than worth it. I wouldn't change a thing.

It's two in the afternoon on a Friday and I'm headed home. I won't be going back into town until sometime Monday, and honestly, if I had my way, I wouldn't even then. I make a point of always trying to be home around this time every day. I don't want to miss it. Ana has no idea the hoops I jump through just so I can be here in time to watch her nurse our son. As I round the corner to the baby's nursery, I stop as the breath stalls in my chest.

Ana is humming a song and our child is suckling from her breast, greedily eating. The little grunts he makes fills the room and I smile, but my heart is full. In this room is my world. My complete world. I once thought love didn't exist, merely survival. I was so fucking wrong. There are no words.

Love exists. I look at Ana now and I can't believe it. I was an asshole. Hell, I still am, in many ways. I used her. I demanded her acceptance, her allegiance, and her body. I held her brother over her head and demanded she give me everything I wanted. I wanted to dominate and own her. My, how the mighty fall. I might have been unfair to her, but in the end, it was her who got the victory.

She owns me. She controls my world.

"I love you, Ana." I tell her and her face jerks up, realizing I'm standing beside her. At my words, tears spring from her eyes. She cries at the drop of a hat these days. I worried about it until she told me that her heart was so full, she couldn't help it.

"I love you, Roman," she whispers, smiling.

Love isn't about survival. I made demand after unjustified demand, trying to own and control what no man could. Love isn't about taking. Love is all about giving. My Ana taught me that, and I'll spend the rest of my life showing her I learned the lesson well.

The End.

AUTHOR'S NOTE

I hope you guys enjoyed Roman and Ana's story. I am already working on a new book and if you like Alpha men claiming their woman hard and fast I think you'll like it. It will be released much fast than this book. You can look for it in May! Turn the page for a sample of my first book Unlawful Seizure if you haven't read it. It's available for 99 cents and free in Kindle Unlimited. You can follow me at any of the links below for more information and keep up to date on what's happening!

Baylee

Author Links:

Baylee Rose Web Page
Baylee Rose Facebook Page
Instagram
Twitter

Sign up for my Newsletter!
Sneak Peeks, Contests and Much More!

Ruthless, Demanding, Wicked and Running from the Law.

Tessa:

It was a routine parole hearing, until I get caught in the middle of a prison break.

Now I'm property of Max Kincaid, Florida Correctional Inmate Number 91428

I should be terrified.

I should be demanding my freedom.

Instead I'm begging him to deliver on all the wicked promises in his eyes.

The longer I'm with him, the more I need him.

His touch answers cravings I never knew my body had.

Now, all I crave is him.

Max:

My life ended years ago.

I have no right to touch Tessa. I should let her go.

I can't. Instead, I lose myself in her body.

I'm living on borrowed time.

But when the devil comes to collect his due,

It will be with her taste on my mouth.

My brand on her body.

And her name on my lips.

This Book is a standalone containing one hot alpha and the woman who wants him even more than the cops chasing them both.

Insta-love, hot *fun* in the Flordia Sun...or rain and a Happily Ever After guaranteed.

236

UNLAWFUL SEIZURE

1

Tess

I wake up with a migraine and feeling sick to my stomach. That is sign number one. Sign number two is my horoscope warning me I shouldn't leave the house today. Sign number three is when I go outside to discover my old, beat up, 1990 something model Toyota, sitting on a flat. I'm stressed out already, and it's only 7 am. I'm all set to call in sick when my boss calls me with his usual song and dance. *I'm sick today Tessa. I really need to take the day off. Clear all my appointments. Make up some excuse for me.* What he really means, is he and his wife are flying to Tahoe for the weekend. I know because Claire, the other secretary, let that little tidbit slip.

When I remind him that Judge Ryson appointed him as counsel in a case that was on the docket this morning, he goes silent. When I inform him it is a parole hearing and can't be rescheduled, that sick feeling only increases. When he asks me to get Stuart to cover for him, we begin a ten-minute conversation on why Stuart is hopeless and will end up losing the case and destroying a man's chance for freedom.

I'm not usually so concerned, but his client today is Max Kincaid, and I'm more than slightly obsessed with this case. Max deserves someone who will actually try to get him free.

I shouldn't be that concerned with this case. I should have kept my fat mouth shut because the next thing I know, Charles, my boss, has volunteered me to go before the parole board and present the case as his proxy. I try every way in the world to stress that I can't do it. I point out that Mr. Kincaid was unlawfully put in jail, and he needs a real attorney looking out for him. I might as well have saved my breath. His response was that I know the case better than anyone and Mr. Kincaid would best be served with me, by his side.

"Tess you know the law inside and out. You can do this." *Click.*

That's the only response I get from my final plea for him to do what the freaking state pays him to do. I really should have quit this job ages ago. I haven't because I can't afford to. I would have loved to go on to law school, but I put myself through school to get my paralegal license. There's no way I can work full time to pay back student loans, and go back to school.

I was stupid enough to think that I would get a job right out of school. Well, not completely stupid. I did get a job immediately—at McDonald's and then later at Shoe Warehouse and Dollar Mart. I had three jobs and still could barely manage to pay rent on my apartment. It was also an apartment I barely visited, unless it was to collapse on the bed to nap before my next shift started.

I was drowning in debt from school loans and so tired I could barely hold my eyes open. When I walked into Charles Barger's, and he offered me a paralegal position, it seemed like the answer to my dreams.

It turned out to be a nightmare.

It does keep a roof over my head though and the damn collection calls down. That's what I remind myself of again today, as I put on my big girl panties and suck it up. It's a parole hearing and on a case I do, in fact, know inside and out.

I get my tire changed and head to the office, grabbing the files and things I will need for the hearing, then head straight for the federal prison in Ormond. It takes a good hour to drive there, and the hearing is scheduled to start in forty minutes. That's when yet another sign from the universe falls in my lap, in the form of a speeding ticket. *Fuck my life!*

I try to pay attention to my speedometer the rest of the trip, but it's hard. My mind is swirling as I go over the facts I need to present to the panel. My boss wasn't lying when he said that I knew this case better than anyone. The truth is I've been consumed with Max Kincaid's case. I must have read his file a thousand times. I know it's not healthy. *I do.* I just can't seem to make myself stop. I stare at his picture, and something about those dark, inky, onyx eyes call to me. His features seem familiar, even though there's no way that's possible.

I've even memorized his information. Max Kincaid, age thirty-six, date of birth February 11, 1979. Dark black hair, black eyes, and three distinct scars. A small one above his right eyebrow, one on his side from an appendectomy he had as a teen, and one jagged scar on his chest he received in the line of duty as a soldier in the Middle East. Max is a hero, awarded the Purple Heart for heroism in battle when he saved his entire platoon from a mortar attack by driving straight into the line of fire and drawing it away from his men. He had more men offer to stand up for him during his murder trial than the judge would allow to testify. By all accounts, Max was the golden boy, the man that women loved, and men wanted to be. His downfall came from loving the wrong woman, marrying her, expecting a child with her and then brutally extracting revenge for their deaths.

I lay awake at night recounting the facts of the case, and having my heart hurt for the man who lost so much, because of a decision filled with revenge. Truthfully, I'm not sure I wouldn't have tried to do the same thing as he did if I were in his shoes. A part of me cheers for him. That's why I'm doing this; but find myself a little giddy at the chance to actually meet Max Kincaid and be close to him.

Claire, my co-worker, likes to joke that I'm halfway in love with the man. If she knew some of the dreams I've had, that involve Max, she'd be ready to call the men in white coats.

This is important. This could be the single most important thing I ever do. Not only will I get to meet the man, but I also get the chance to be the one to right a wrong. Yes, he killed a man, and yes, that is wrong. However, the circumstances of the case, the outstanding character witnesses that testified on his behalf and the fact that he has already served five years of his sentence without a single demerit or mark against him, all combine and tell me he should get parole. Now, if I can just convince the court of that.

I feel strongly that he was wronged. I think I'm supposed to do this. *I'm supposed to be the one to rescue him.* That's the real reason why I ignore the signs the universe keeps throwing my way. It's also why I don't let the fear that floods me when I drive through the prison gates, after checking in at the guardhouse, overpower me.

I go through all of the security points at the main entrance and have my files, purse and items searched. I manage only to be five minutes late, but in the end that doesn't matter since a couple members of the panel are running behind. That will give me a few minutes to meet with Max...I mean Mr. Kincaid before the hearing and go over our battle plan.

"Could you have Mr. Kincaid brought down now? I'd like to meet with him before our hearing."

"You'll have to wait here until I have the prisoner brought in and settled," the guard tells me.

"I...okay. That's fine. I'll just wait here." He doesn't reply and goes out.

My heart is beating out of my chest. I need to move past my excitement of getting to meet Max Kincaid and get my mind onto obtaining his freedom for him. It's another ten minutes; which only serves to increase my nerves, before the guard comes back and escorts me in. For a minute, I think I stop breathing. Max is sitting at a table, and if I ignore the orange jumpsuit, he looks even better than he did in his pictures. His black hair is straight and lays lazily on his head, making it look like someone has lovingly run their fingers through it. His dark eyes pin me immediately and with such intensity it takes all I have not to hesitate when walking towards him. His large hands are lying on the table with chains around them. I know that is normal procedure, but on him it feels wrong.

I don't know what I imagined our first words would be to each other. In my daydreams of Max, I thought we'd meet, and I'd rescue him and he'd be the *one*. The man who would understand me, who would just…*fit me*. I thought somewhere in the deep recesses of my mind he might recognize that feeling when he saw me for the first time, too. It sounds all kinds of stupid and juvenile and normally I'm not that kind of woman. I don't know why I am where Max is concerned.

All of those wishes and silly dreams are blown out of the water when his harsh, barking voice rings out and stops me in my tracks.

"Who the fuck are you?"

2

Max

I've given up on hope. Hope doesn't exist. It hasn't since five years ago when I heard the sound of cold metal slamming shut, and I began my stay at the Ormond County Correctional and Rehabilitation Institution. Hope left that day, and it hasn't returned. Life took on the dull gray color of the prison itself, and I became a creature who didn't live. I only existed.

Today is my parole hearing. My fourth to be exact. It doesn't mean shit. They're not going to set me free. That doesn't happen when you kill a man. I don't give a fuck. I find I don't give a fuck about anything these days. I haven't in a long time. I won't get parole because every time a bunch of stiff-necked suits ask me if I feel remorse for my crime, I laugh.

I killed the man who murdered my wife. She was a whore. I didn't love her, didn't even like her. But I did love the child she was carrying. So I hunted him down, and I squeezed the life out of him with my bare hands. I watched as, bit by bit, the light drained from his eyes and just when he was about to die, I let the pressure off his neck and allowed him to gasp another breath. Then, I did it again. Rinse and repeat until finally I ended the motherfucker. I relished it. I spit on his corpse as I let him fall to the ground. I didn't feel remorse. *Shit, no.* Instead, I got the first fucking hard on I'd had in months.

A machine-made sound buzzes and the retracting of my cell door begins. I stand there as Officer Jenkins comes into view. He's a cocky asshole who gets his kicks out of beating prisoners, just because he can. I tower over him. Hell, I could snap him like a fucking twig. I've always restrained but as he looks at me a sneer on his face and spits at my shoes, I can't help but wonder if two murders would send me to hell quicker? It might be worth the gamble.

"Let's go, cupcake. Time for you to go and beg for freedom like the candy-ass you are," he says, grabbing my arm and pulling me in front of him.

I don't say anything; I don't even change my facial expression. This piss-ant ain't nothing to me. If I liked him, even marginally, I'd warn him there is a prison riot and break out planned for today. I might even go one step further and tell him he's the one Hernandez, and his crew are planning on beating the shit out of. Hell, I'd even warn him about the jagged Coke bottle they had smuggled in and have been fixing up, just for his lily white ass. I don't. The ass-reaming he's going to get couldn't happen to a nicer guy. We walk down a long hall, surrounded by prison cells on each side. I ignore the yelling, questions, and catcalls. I have a reputation as someone you do not fuck with, in this joint. That's good enough for me. Hernandez tried to get me to join his crew for the breakout. I didn't. There's nothing waiting for me outside these doors. *Not a fucking thing.*

We make our way to the last set of steel doors, and they slide open as the guard on the other side lets us in. I'm escorted into an elevator where another guard joins us. I forget this one's name. Byron or something like that, pretty decent guy. I'd warn him, but then he'd feel obligated to stop it, and that wouldn't be good for me. So I don't. My conscience has been colored gray like these fucking walls, too.

The small room where they hold the parole hearings hasn't changed; neither has the smell. The smell of the prison permeates every inch of the place. If there is one thing I fucking hate the most about this place, it is the stink of it.

I'm placed at a small table that will face the panel. It's a familiar routine. There will be a bunch of tight assed, fancy dressed assholes, who look as if my presence offends them. Hell, they need to get in line. My presence offends my own damn self.

I'm waiting for everyone to show up when *she* walks in.

Fucking hell! Who let her in here? She walks through the door looking lost. *She is.* She's a damned baby thrown into an angry tank of sharks. She's going to get eaten alive. She has hair the color of coffee, creamy and rich. It's pulled on top of her head and wrapped in a bun. I'm sure it was meant to give her a matronly appearance. It does not. It exposes her neck and makes the beast in me want to bite into it while I bend her over the damn table she just put the briefcase on. She's wearing black, dress pants that hug her slim thighs and a red silk shirt. I can't even remember the last time I had sex and one look at her, and my dick is ready to come for days. Come all over her, to be exact. A picture of her buck-ass naked and covered in my jizz, from her thick apple lips to her fuck-me stilettos, cements in my mind.

"Who the fuck are you?" I bark at her, annoyed at the way my dick is standing at attention.

"I...I'm Mr. Barger's paralegal," she stumbles, her eyes widen in surprise, with a healthy dose of fear mixed in when she looks at me.

"Who the fuck is Mr. Barger?" I ask, doing my best to ignore the way her shirt exposes the mounds of her breasts when she bends over to look through her papers.

"Your lawyer, he was unavoidably detained. I'm here to stand in..."

"I don't have a fucking lawyer!"

"The court appointed Mr. Barger to appear on your behalf. Now, if you'll give me just a few minutes, we can get started. There are some things I'd like to go over with you before I address the panel."

"I don't want you addressing the panel," I respond, and when it appears like she's going to argue with me, I look at the guard who stayed to monitor me. "I don't want her talking on my behalf. I want her *gone*."

"Really Mr. Kincaid, if you would just…"

"Lady, my name is Max or Inmate number 91428, not Mr. Kincaid."

"Fine, Mr. Kincaid, I mean Max, if you will just allow me to…"

"I don't want counsel! I *decline* it. Now get the hell out."

The guard finally stands up. Maybe he'll actually do something. I need this little lamb out of here before the animals start to attack and eat her alive. She needs to be gone before we go into a full-blown riot. It would appear my conscious is not totally dead.

"Is there a problem?" The guard asks. If I weren't worried about getting this chick out of here, I'd stop to roll my fucking eyes.

"Not at all officer. Please have a seat," the woman interjects. "Now as I was saying, Mr. Barger was called out of town with an emergency. I am the one in the office most familiar with your case, and he sent me in his place. I'm Tessa Oliver, now if we could get started."

"It would appear that the prisoner does not want your counsel, Ms. Oliver," the guard says.

Gee ya think? Dumbass.

"No, he just didn't realize…"

"Damn straight I don't," I interrupt before she can finish.

She looks back at me with shock, and there's a fiery glint in her eyes that tells me I've just pissed her off. That might have been interesting had the alarm not sounded right then. She looks in the direction of the noise.

"What is…?" She asks. The guard, who already knows what

the alarm means, breaks every rule in his training and runs out of the small room, leaving me alone with the woman.

"What's going on?" She questions again, and this time she looks pale and scared. *She should.* I take a deep breath.

I didn't want this. I have no fucking use for the game that's about to be played. It's too late; the die has been cast. If I leave her on her own, she will be dead or wishing for death by nightfall. I stand up. I'd be lying if I said my dick wasn't twitching at the way I tower over her small, delicate frame, or at the way her eyes widen in real fear as she tries to step back from me. My hands are in shackles so I do the only thing I can. I take them both and lift them over her head and pull her back into me, letting the heavy chains rest on her chest and against her neck.

"You have just become a prisoner in a prison break."

Her cry of fear competes with my growl of anger.

Fuck.

Made in the USA
San Bernardino, CA
01 August 2018